Southword *45*

Southword is published
by Southword Editions
an imprint of the
Munster Literature Centre
Frank O'Connor House
84 Douglas Street
Cork City T12 X802
Ireland

www.munsterlit.ie

@MunLitCentre

/southwordjournal

/munsterliteraturecentre

#Southword

Issue 45
ISBN 978-1-915573-06-3

Editor
Patrick Cotter

Fiction Editor
Billy O'Callaghan

Production
James O'Leary

Thank you to Anne Kennedy for her technical assistance

The opinions expressed by contributing writers are not necessarily representative of the publisher's or editors' opinions

Cover image: *'Firkin Crane'* by Anne Kennedy

The Munster Literature Centre is a grateful recipient of funding from

CONTENTS

Please Subscribe

By subscribing, you will receive new issues of *Southword* straight from the printers, as quickly as we will ourselves. Your subscription will also help to provide us with the resources to make *Southword* even better.

Rates for two issues per year:

Ireland, UK, North America, Australia, New Zealand	€20 *postage free*
Rest of Europe	€24 *postage free, tax-inclusive*
Rest of the World	€30 *postage included*

For subscriptions and renewals visit www.munsterlit.ie – payment accepted by PayPal.

Southword may also be purchased issue-by-issue through Amazon outlets worldwide and select book shops in Ireland, the UK, Europe and the USA.

Amidst Fierce Flames

A First-Hand Dissection of Anger and Its Fiery Consequences

Eleanor Ariadne Shaw

1st Prize, Southword Literary Essay Competition

I am seated on a speedy, excessively air-conditioned train, darting clumsily through the Czech countryside. The tracks are surrounded by tall, forested hills on either side, and the morning mist has lifted to reveal a pale blue sky dotted with velvety frail-looking clouds. The fierce July sun, of which the small country has not, unfortunately, been spared, beats down on the landscape of interchanging fields and villages, its rays reflected by the minute drops of dew which cover the ground like individual stitches of a vast blanket of moisture.

A smartly dressed, lanky youngster – scarcely older than twenty-five – passes my seat for the fourth time, dragging behind him a rackety trolley filled to the brim with packaged food and drinks, including several flavours of beef jerky, a delicacy the Czechs seem particularly drawn to. His presence is announced by a pungent odour of cheap instant coffee, and lingers languidly in the air for a few moments after he has gone. A sallow-faced woman pointedly buries her nose behind a handkerchief as he passes, and yet a faint smile is etched onto her gaunt, pinched cheekbones as our glances meet. Imperceptibly, an instant, unspoken connection passes between us, of warmth and forgiveness and sunshine and perhaps even of the absurdity of it all. It seems entirely bizarre, then, to know that the external tranquillity revealed nothing of the smouldering temper I felt inside. The anger had consumed me entirely as I darted through Eastern Europe that summer, burning and implacable. Naturally, as would anyone who spent their days strolling by the glistening waters of the Danube or admiring Plečnik's vibrant Ljubljana, I also experienced a great deal of happiness and gratitude. Nonetheless, it was that peculiar and illogical emotion which complemented the holiday least – the anger – which undeniably stood out.

Again, the sun blazes down on me, blinding me, and yet a stinging flash of cold erupts on the nape of my neck and travels down my spine. The notoriously forceful German rain drums against the large windows enclosing the conference room, drowning out the polite murmurings of its occupants. Sitting down, I raise the piece of paper I have just read from above my head to shield my eyes from the glaring, clinical lights suspended from the ceiling.

It reads: "Condemning the West's Actions in Libya, a Proposal for Resolution II". I'm sure the speech had gone well, as had the general debate, but once again I felt unable to partake in my teammate's hushed, excited whisperings. The familiar flicker of irritation, the burning sensation which clawed mercilessly at my stomach had returned, and my head pulsed with repressed rage.

I am often angry when discussing or reading about politics, as I'm sure many people are, and for good reason. I get angry at the fact that endless debates like the aforementioned can be had and the topic never repeated, due to the sheer amount of vile atrocities which occur daily. I am angry that a handful possess too much power and most too little. I get angry at the world and my inability to change it.

It was anger which propelled me through my schooling, a near incessant swelling and scattered waning of fury which impelled me to work long hours on maths papers and essays. My mother has said for as long as I can remember that the panacea for unwanted emotions is to "get up and do something", and yet my anger has seemed to stubbornly persist throughout everything I was doing, hanging over me like a crackling storm cloud in an old cartoon.

***

There appears to exist a belief, promoted from my experience largely by the impervious older generations, that a dazzling new age has dawned upon our civilisation in the last decade, allowing us more freedom of expression than ever before. This stands in contrast to the emotional, psychological, and – by extension – literary dark ages they grew up in, in which radical sentiments and offensive passions were diligently concealed. And while it is undoubtedly true that the widespread freedom we are able to enjoy now used to be scarce, it is misleading to assume that our generalised perception of "unwanted" emotions such as anger have particularly changed.

"5 Facts About a Woman's Anger to Help Control it", "6 Tips to Tame Your Everyday Temper", "You're Not Angry – You're Weak", "Try relaxation techniques – deep breathing and picturing happy scenes".

These tantalising headlines are imbued within the pages of most online newspapers and lifestyle magazines – targeted especially at women – and are an excellent representation of societal attitudes on anger. One should not hesitate to express and exult in their fleeting, surface-level manifestations of frustration, as they can be swiftly and equally superficially "fixed" to last until the next inevitable outburst. The brooding, ever-present frustration lurking just below the surface must stay there, hidden and ignored – "Focus on gratitude!" – as it is both too complex and too inconvenient to "fix".

Contrary to my own beliefs, however, this discourse on how to address and regard anger is not new – in fact it was a point of contention among the ancients, too.

"Anybody can become angry, that is easy; but to be angry [...] for the right purpose, and in the right way, that is not within everybody's power, that is not easy." So argued Aristotle in the 4th century B.C.E.

"We shouldn't control anger, but destroy it entirely – for what control is there for a thing that's fundamentally wicked?" replies Seneca – not physically of course, unless his training in rhetoric included conversing with the dead.

These two starkly contrasting perspectives on anger form a theoretical groundwork for a subject I was keen to explore from a young age, ever since my otherwise rather uneventful existence was interrupted by the initial surge of blistering rage. It goes without saying that anger is no deferential servant. So, I felt I needed to pick apart my anger, layer by layer, and understand it, with the fanciful hope of eventually being able to work with it rather than be stuck in the throes of an unwinnable fight against it.

***

The Seven Deadly Sins and the Four Last Things, ostensibly by Dutch painter Hieronymus Bosch, was my favourite of the many splendid artworks I saw one sweltering summer afternoon at the Prado in Madrid. If you stand far enough away and squint slightly, perhaps tilting your head to one side to provide your bizarre gestures with an academic air, you might notice the shape in the painting resembling an eye. The eye – so it is said – belongs to God. In the pupil is a miniature painting of Christ emerging from the tomb, but it is the surrounding seven images, comprising a rather colourful iris, which prove particularly interesting. Wrath is easily the most noticeable of the seven sins, depicted rather crudely at the lowest point of the iris as an animated fight between two drunken peasants. As I see it, this portrayal encapsulates perfectly the wholly negative Christian perception of anger which has pervaded much of history, and, as it happens, much of my own life. "[Our thinking] was based largely on the idea that reason and the emotions, or passions, as they were called, were at war and the task of the Christian was to subject the passions to the control of reason," says Bill Cosgrave in the article *Understanding Anger.*

This idea calls to mind bittersweet memories, fleeting moments from my childhood, of shafts of golden sunlight dancing and diving off of the shabby front terrace and my great-grandmother's steely gaze fixated upon me. The air around her buzzed with the electricity of perturbed glances and Orthodox platitudes left unspoken. Tufts of dying yellowish grass swayed rhythmically in the quickening breeze like the plucking of strings on a soundless harp, and I sensed that they, too, felt as I did inside. When she did speak, hands balled into fists and positioned decisively upon both hips, my great-grandmother would belabour the importance of living an appreciative, Christian life and resisting the immoral temptations of rage. She paused only to sigh dolefully to herself and sip at her ouzo, whereupon she launched headlong into her tirade with renewed vigour.

Admittedly, it is not only the Christian religion which promotes such a cynical stance on anger. I found the Buddhist teachings of the Theravāda schools to be particularly interesting, which "unquestionably [reject] anger, in any and all forms. One of the ways that the canonical tradition represents the harm of anger is to tell us that anger makes us ugly" (Carol S. Anderson and *Anger Makes Us Ugly: Reflections from Pāli Buddhism*). This unique notion is taken one step further, with the claim – again from Anderson's work – that angry people "will be reborn in the hells, due to their misconduct with speech, mind, and body."
It is unsurprising, then, that I have always lived with a perpetual, nagging fear that – whichever religion happens to ultimately be the "correct" one – I will go to whatever version of hell corresponds to it. It seems irrelevant that I try desperately to quell the anger, and certainly that I very rarely act on it, as if its mere existence is justification enough.

***

In Honolulu, Hawaii – the racially-divided, US-Navy dominated Hawaii of 1932, that is – a series of events occurred which put another nail in the coffin for those who desperately clung onto the ideal of Hawaii as the progressive melting pot of the United States. These events, rather unexpectedly, provided me with a most intriguing perspective regarding my own circumstances. A white naval sailor named Deacon Jones admits in an interview with Peter van Slingerland that he was responsible for the death of Kahahawai, a Hawaiian man accused of playing a role in the violent kidnapping of Thalia Massie, the wife of a fellow navy officer. The original trial – which dealt with the kidnapping itself – had caused an island-wide uproar. Towering stone walls snaking their way over the lush undergrowth of the islands were initially intended to keep the Natives away from the Navy employees. Now they served the opposite purpose, and protected native Hawaiians from ruthless public attacks. Impossibly, the second trial based on the confession provided in the aforesaid interview was even more contentious, and the story rapidly became a national headline. Deacon Jones and the other officers who were present as the shot was fired were charged with murder and sentenced to ten years in prison, with the implication that Jones' behaviour had been racially motivated. Nationwide rage followed, oozing out of the ever-deepening cracks in the brittle shell that remained of the American justice system. Ten years in prison became sixty minutes.
During this infamous interview, Jones denies any animosity directed at Kahahawai by saying, "Well I don't hate anybody. Hate is another expression of fear" (transcript to be found in the brilliant book "*Black Rage Confronts the Law*" by Paul Harris). This concept is not new, and it is also often argued that hatred is a byproduct of anger, which suggests

that anger must be inextricably linked with either palpable or subconscious feelings of fear. In fact, fear has permeated this entire story from start to finish. Native Hawaiians – driven by decades of injustice – feared the outright withdrawal of their already restricted rights, and reacted by furiously clashing with the equally angry Navy officers, who – in turn – feared for the erosion of their dominating presence on the island. This realisation of weakening power, of an imbalance which slowly ceased to be the social norm, may also have been the defining factor for Deacon Jones in the violent killing of Joseph Kahahawai. Distress and terror are deeply ingrained in the individual folds and crevices of our social fabric. Friendships are frequently formed on the basis of common fears – and, therefore, common targets for anger – and it needn't be said how many animosities stemming from mutual fear result in the release of rampant fury. Of course, I am not comparing like with like when I discuss these events in connection to my own feelings – my anger is nothing like Jones' – and yet it was upon reading this story many years ago that I first made this seemingly obvious connection. I realise now what a ridiculously simple association this was to make, and shamed myself for not having made it sooner. It is severely difficult, I have discovered, to confess to oneself how scared one really is. It was as uncomplicated as that – a primary explanation for the irrational wrath which spilled out of me was the largely rational fear that still boiled and bubbled within me. I fear the world, and am therefore angry at it, and I am angry that I have to be constantly afraid of the world to survive.

When I think of the safe, unchallenged life I have led so far, free of hardship and worries of any kind, it frustrates me that not all young people were able to enjoy the same privileges. A natural reaction, I should think – a sort of survivor's guilt without the death. It scares me that not everyone had my kind, gentle, supportive parents who gave me a life rife with opportunities in which I could flourish and function as I pleased. I've often observed in people, including myself, the willingness to adopt the problems of others as one's own and partake in the suffering they are forced to endure, thereby causing one's own confidence and happiness to gradually whittle away. Fear and anger are multiplied, in a sense, and are not all your own. The young person's notion of inactivity, of being constantly behind and having wasted away the developmental years, is another fear-inducing idea in which feelings of anger thrive. After all, Cosgrave defines anger as being "energy for action", an emotional or physical arousal and yearning for change. Unlike young Tolstoy who "wasted" away his early years in the era-appropriate medium of drinking and gambling on his vast estate, I spend inordinate amounts of time online. Sometimes I am tempted to be bitter about this, but then remember I am no Tolstoy.

***

This societally promoted idea of having wasted away my prime years, as well as the egregious sequence of events I mention above, briefly touch on a theory I feel is worth exploring in more depth. Controversial as it is, the idea that anger and other such "unpleasant" emotions are not necessarily isolated individual matters, but are almost always a result of larger societal problems, has often been used as a scapegoat for those unwilling to confront their own feelings. "I blame society; Society's to blame; I claim society; Is playing a hostile game" – so the indie band Titus Andronicus in their eponymous song *(I Blame) Society*. However, when watered down to the key pillars upon which the structure of society is built, it is easy to see why this claim stands to reason. Humans are, by nature, community creatures living within the boundaries of communal systems, who possess the ability to learn about the plight of fellow humans continents away and subsequently internalise this emotion, who share many of the same feelings of anger and resentment upon realising that their community has turned against them.

Last winter I found myself in Heptonstall, a minute village of dappled greyish brick nestled in a small valley in West Yorkshire. Though the quaint tea room and large, frosty windows adorning shadowy façades proved infinitely more attractive than I had imagined, the true reason for my coming lurked between tall tufts of dying grass in the far corner of the dusty village cemetery. The placement of Sylvia Plath's grave had seemed odd to me then, curiously out of place among rows of identical headstones in the dreary graveyard of a rural parish. The only detail that set hers apart was a winding path of well trodden grass which led directly to a footstone adorned with scattered poppies. As I stood alone in this dismal place, hands in pockets to keep out the biting wind, I couldn't help but think of all the other people who had stood where I stood, paying tribute to this singularly important poet. Though I have passed the inevitable stage in the life of a book-loving, teenage girl during which I obsessed over her melodramatic writing, I still thoroughly enjoy her work, and have only recently come to realise the intensity and vibrance which dominates much of it.

Plath was the first poet I read who could truthfully etch onto a page some of the anger I felt. Upon listening to the BBC recordings of 1962, in which Plath read aloud the poems from her collection *Ariel*, author Megan Abbot was surprised not to hear "something more ethereal, a doomy Ophelia floating down the river." In fact: "There was, instead, something ferocious about them." In 1966, a reviewer discussing a poem from this same collection argued: "What is more, *Daddy* was merely the first jet of flame from a literary dragon who in the last months of her life breathed a burning river of bile across the literary landscape." It was Plath's depiction of anger, especially when discussing feminist ideas which, among other things, made her such a controversial figure in the literary world. Feminine suffering has historically been viewed as an inescapable aspect of female existence, the idea that women experience a form of "built-in" pain, a concept which of course is dependent

entirely upon the continued presence of the patriarchal system. This pain must, however, be expressed in a seemly and feminine manner – ever-silent, calm, and alluring throughout. Much like the troubled Ophelia – a woman whose many betrayals lead to insurmountable heartbreak – who submits herself to a non-violent, beautiful, and graceful suicide.
The painting by Millais portrays this figure rather well, the subject's hands in a pose of submission, accepting of her fate, and enduring faithfulness symbolised by the ring of violets around her neck. A woman's anger is undesirable and manly, especially if directed towards the oppressive system itself; an unpleasant and shameful inconvenience.

Despite this, a frequently referenced term in discussions surrounding the subject of feminist frustration is the "anger window", and how a culmination of centuries of obediently suppressed rage has caused the window to break open, with the panes of injustice dangling limply by their hinges. In other words, women are now able to be publicly angry, without needing to suppress their unfavourable emotions to appease their male counterparts. In all honesty, I have always struggled coming to terms with such a theory. It follows that the opportunity for women to increasingly be true to themselves and release their frustrations – the "anger window", as it were – must be linked to the metaphorical closing of the door of inequality and hatred and violence. Clearly, this is not the case. Just recently I had the pleasure of watching a livestream of a protest in Athens calling for the release of internet personality and professional misogynist Andrew Tate, who had been imprisoned in Romania on charges of rape and human trafficking. The vitriolic hatred he spewed when confronted with capable, independent women amassed thousands of adoring fans. Is it enough for this open "anger window" to merely exist, when the response to any woman's nonconformist actions has been unchanged?
While it is certainly true to say that the simple fact that women are able to publicly express themselves outside of traditional gender roles is significant progress, the reasons for and the results of this anger are eerily unaffected. Historically, a woman's fury has bubbled incessantly and constantly under the befitting exterior of a traditional lady. Contemporarily, the anger finds release in the form of occasional scorching outbursts which begin with the temporary slipping of society's veil of respect and end abruptly once a woman is told to "get over it".
This new age of "outspokenness" does not only apply to feminist concerns, and can be observed in the increased dissemination of weighty talking points such as climate change. Though, while it is true that the discussion surrounding it has increased exponentially, climate change has only really been in the public conscience for the last century or so, while women's oppression has existed for millenia (which is not to say, of course, that climate change is of lesser importance, seeing as it is likely to eventually wipe us all out either way).

***

"Even Amidst Fierce Flames/The Golden Lotus Can Be Planted". Ted Hughes claimed that this quote, which would become the inscription for his wife's headstone, was plucked from the pages of ancient Hindu scriptures. My amateur research, combined with the studies of more adept experts, proved otherwise: the quotation likely stems from a tale by the sixteenth century Chinese novelist and poet, Wu Cheng'en, in which a Patriarch is preaching the means to achieving a long life. In conjunction with my own musings on anger, two interpretations can be extracted from this rather vague assertion. Firstly, even in a furious state – when one is "amidst fierce flames" – one can survive, nay, flourish even. Anger is not, therefore, a purely unpleasant, destruction-nurturing emotion. Alternatively, the Patriarch speaks of the importance of guarding one's "vital powers", such as the spirit and the soul, and how when these are kept under close control, even a seemingly unsalvageable emotion such as rage gives way to progress, an interpretation which regards this emotion in a purely negative light.

I have always struggled to accurately describe my unabating frustration, ebbing and flowing like the tide in a rather dangerous bay, but I feel the phrase "amidst fierce flames" summarises it well. I remember experiencing this same sense of recognition, of being truly understood, when I first heard Tchaikovsky's 1812 Overture. I was a young, bright-eyed girl then, clinging to the coarse, cushioned seat at the Alte Oper in Frankfurt. As the piece nears the finale, the orchestra becomes harsher and more vigorous, and an unbearable tension clings to every surface. The cannons suddenly shatter this temporary sensation of weightless discomfort, sounding out in crazed desperation and dissonance. A feeling of infinite relief at being rid of the all-consuming suffocating feeling washes over the hall, weaving skilfully in between seats and up stairs until it has been tangibly felt by every person in the audience. The heat and blinding light of an erupting volcano engulfs the hall. Then, in the blink of an eye, in the time it takes to strum a deep eighth note on the enormous double bass in the back row, the feeling vanishes. A slow, imposing march fills the emptiness, bringing with it a dreadful realisation which settles in the soul like fine ash and poisonous soot, falling drearily from the heavens. Everything will remain the same, the status quo will persist, nothing will change. Every time the piece is played — and I've gone to hear it a couple of times since — I can't help but feel a strange strand of unrealistic hope wrapped tightly around my neck, for what exactly I don't know. Nevertheless, despite the multitude of personal alterations the conductor may impose, the score he conducts remains unchanged. The same growing tension, the same eruption of emotion, the same sinking feeling which follows. This is what my anger is. So, what now? What is the solution, if one exists?

In all likelihood the ultimate answer, as with so many things in life, is balance. Precariously balancing the tightrope which separates unbridled fury from utter apathy is challenging, not to speak of having to repeat the process day in and day out, yet I believe it must be done. Alice A. Keefe summarises a similar argument promoted by writers such as Audre

Lorde and Anita Burrows by saying that they "suggest the work of 'tending the fire' of anger with discernment and awareness is an essential, albeit daunting, spiritual task." Virtue and beauty can be found in the functionality of anger; it exists, after all, to serve a precise psychological purpose. In essence:

"My anger has meant pain to me but it has also meant survival and before I give it up I am going to make sure there is something at least as powerful on the road to clarity."
— Audre Lorde's "The Uses of Anger: Women Responding to Racism"

The truth is that the phenomenon of anger is messy and complex; simultaneously bewildering and utterly simple; an emotion which either brings one out of oneself, violently and unnervingly, or protects one, by acting as a necessary warning. Even if we acknowledge that anger may be both positive or negative, constructive and destructive, it is impossible to categorise specific instances of anger as inherently good or bad. My anger is an inalienable part of me, tethered to me like my limbs are to my body and my heart is to my soul. Regardless of whether it will accompany me through life or not, I mustn't let it consume me; after all, it is chained to me and not I to it. A distinction which makes the world of a difference.

Why Plant a Flag at the Pole?

Devon Balwit

For Scott's polar party, *late* meant *lost,*
meant *dead.* When I'm late, I'm surely lost

to the dog. Dead he doesn't know, only less
of me, a waning till what's left is scentless.

Late students lose most of my intention.
Late too often, and despite my best intentions,

they die to me. I'm only human and prone
to holding grudges. Just as a student, prone

across the desk, phone in hand, is dead
weight for those of us man-hauling. The dead

are little more than backdrop for our myths.
Scott, the heroic gentleman, was one such myth.

Closer scrutiny proved him petulant and wrong
when rightness mattered most. Perhaps it's wrong

to judge the late, the lost, the dead. The storm
won't quit. We make no headway in our storms.

Cochlea

Faye Boland

Give me a gastropod, *babbalucci*
whorled shell to retreat into.

Shellakybooky refuge from wind's bite,
the sting of hail and rain.

A spiral haven
echoing my *caracol* breath.

Let me slumber here in coiled aragonite
until I am ready for the slow

slide towards my *schnecke* purpose,
a glistening ribbon slithering behind.

Cult of Artemis

Despy Boutris

— *Diana and Actaeon,* Titian

& today I'm back at the ruined lake.
Today I'm back on my back, held
by brackish water that touches

even the untouched parts of me.
Years ago, a girl & I stripped &
jumped from the rock, tried to tread

with legs entwined, the thrill of heat
against heat. Years ago, a girl & I
caught a man leering from behind

the chain-link: half-unzipped Levi's,
half-obscured hand. The way
his mouth quirked up

when he saw us see him, hand
we could hardly see, old Volvo
following us, one headlight

burned out. & last week,
walking home, two men in a pickup
kept step for half a mile

while I focused on my feet, wished
to dislocate this warped desire
like my shoulder, or to stop turning

to metaphor at the first sign of fear.
The truth is that some days
it's hard to gauge my odds

at survival, & some days
I'm anything but brave. Rusted
chain-link, rusted wheel rims.

After dark—sky a blend of violets—
I know better now than to reach
for a girl's hand. O let me turn

hunter instead of hunted.
I've spent my whole life being prey.

A Difference of Opinion, Unstated

Kevin Brown

Whenever Mike's grandfather's father
mentioned Irish John, he called him *quare,*
a word I never knew my ancestors knew
until Mike mentioned it, but it echoed
down my family tree until it came to me.

Irish John bought a barely put together
cabin out of the way of others, plugged holes
where cold crept in as if he were solidifying
an argument. He only came to town for
corn meal and milk when he picked up his mail:
manila envelopes and magazines nobody heard tell
of: *Belgravia* and *Blackwood's, The North*
American Review and *Harper's Weekly.*
Quare, they said.

They supposed his supper was cornbread
and the beans he grew in the small garden
that clung to the one window of sunlight,
maybe mixed some pecans, black walnuts,
and chestnuts for lunch, with apples that grew nearby,
no fish or rabbit, not even chickens or their eggs.
Quare, they said.

No interest in dances on Saturday nights
where he might woo a woman or talk
with men about farming or firearms,
punctuated with the sound of spit hitting
the ground, as he watched weekend evenings
from beside a fire reading books that arrived
in boxes, some names they knew, most not:
Collins and Trollope; Douglass and Dostoevsky;
Ibsen and Verlaine; Nietzsche and Zola; some
in languages even the schoolteacher couldn't cipher.
Quare, they said.

Nobody knew how long he lived there—his
accent said he was from somewhere else,
but sounded close enough to be kin—so
nobody knew how many years he lived
before they found him cold in his cabin,
only speculated on how long he lived his life
in such a *quare* way, every day until the
contentment he followed with the
consistency of a clock stopped.
Quare, they said.

Mike gave me the who, what, where,
and when, even speculations on how,
but nobody could answer the *why,*
the *from what cause,* as scholars and
Irish John might say, if he said at all.
Quare, indeed.

A Priest Writes a Letter to Another Priest

Ion Corcos

I'm not a believer in the same god as you. I see
the trail of smoke from the incense burner,
how it shifts like clouds and falls into sky;
if we are all from the same source why
are we living as a desolate archipelago of frogs?

When the woods come alive, it is the leaves,
the birds, worms, grey snakes, the ear listening,
the lichen, silver ragwort, too, that makes it;
it is not the inscriptions on graves, memories.
A ruler set against stone measures its length;

it cannot count the grains within it.
On a walk through flowering black locusts,
bees in their incessant chorus; brother, listen,
if all I do is look, I will not see, and if all I do
is search, I will never find. I may be near,

but must let it come to me. I ask you,
if I push through branches, thorns, to find a bird
I hear singing, will I see it?
Or is it best to sit, stay quiet, wait –
not in thought, then I'll miss it, not eager either.

After a while, I may just find it; the longer I am silent,
the more I will see. This is no sacrifice.

Mrs. Violet Club

Polina Cosgrave

Nuclear lollipops, irresistible bombshells, red-hot babes. Sucking on death is our species' favourite pastime. One has to appreciate all the pretty nicknames found for the weapons of mass destruction. As if they were our lovers.

Look at you, you Violet Club, one hell of a woman! Your sleek plump body, the gleaming chef-d'oeuvre in the caring hands of an engineer. These pictures of you in black and white make the blood boil harder than your charge would, if you were given the chance to be dropped upon our heads.

But you never had one, alas. Oh, how luxurious your flight could have been! We'd yield before you, we'd burn alive with lust forever and ever. But in those days, we liked a bigger girl. Violet Club, poor cutie: hardly a megaton, no thermo- to your nuclear power... You never amounted to anything. Your uncertainty failed you.

Replaced by the new sexy Ms. Red Snow (another dirty fission bomb, dirty, you heard me) like a boring sterile wife, you never cried for your fruitless destiny. In your fantasies you can see your blast radius doubling, tripling, beating the world to a violet pulp.

Are we scared yet? Are we scarred yet? Are we scattered yet?

Niñas
Madeline Beach Carey

When I was first pregnant, I got very good at math. A knack suddenly for numbers. I could calculate percentages faster than anyone at work. Convert miles and feet to metric measurements.

"There must be a little engineer in there," we would joke.

And somehow I thought math meant a boy, that we would have a son. I was terrified. Would my baby try to replace my husband's dead son? I kept dreaming of Joseph, seeing his face as he swam laps. His nose just beneath the surface, one green eye emerging as he turned, effortlessly, to breathe.

At twenty weeks, we found out Elena was a girl, and she was born with dark eyes.

After Elena was born, there was, of course, all that tenderness: the swelling between my legs, the dull ache in my sacrum, the softness of the deflated abdomen. For the first several weeks, it was, as I had feared, as so many women had told me, quite gruesome. I never looked down there, or even felt around for the stitches. At my six-week check-up, when the nurse mentioned tearing of the anal sphincters, I imagined riptide circles, spreading and spreading and spreading again. When I came home, even though the nurse had said all was well, it still felt as if my glute muscles had been ripped from my body, as if all the flesh could just slide off the bones. But, miraculously, by week eight, day one, I began to feel close to normal again. Elena still nursed about once an hour, but my nipples were no longer cracked or sore. All the swelling between my legs was gone, and once, in the deepest darkest part of the night, when Blake was up getting me water and the baby had dozed off, I slipped my finger into my underwear in order to investigate the scar the nurse had mentioned—a spot I was told to massage with rosehip oil twice a day, as if I had time for massages of any sort—and yes, there was a tiny, rough ridge, but there was also the usual slickness: my cunt, the one I had had all my life: damp, mostly smooth, comfortingly familiar.

Other things got normal quickly too.

In the evenings, after eight, when the sun finally went down, we would walk. Sometimes all the way to the ice cream shop on 28th Street, other days just to Wyman Park, where I would sit on a swing and rock Elena in the baby sling, or nurse her while sitting on a bench painted pale blue and stenciled with the now notorious slogan:

BALTIMORE, THE CITY THAT READS. I wore sundresses, no bra. The evenings were brutal that summer. It was always hot and humid, the baby was always bright red. We both had heat rash, but I was happy. Hurting a bit, but happy.

Anyhow, at week eight, day three, we were coming back from the ice cream shop. I had managed to consume half a scoop of rum raisin, but Elena wanted to eat, so I had chucked my cone and begun to nurse her as we walked, breast exposed against a long burnt orange sundress. Someone had given me the dress years earlier, I'd pulled it out of a bag of hand-me-downs and was surprised that it fit. All the pregnancy weight had melted away: I was soft, but back to my old weight. So there I was in the dress, left breast out, Elena wearing nothing but a diaper, when Blake stopped and greeted a couple on our very street. The man was red-headed and holding an old hound dog by the collar. The woman was dark-haired, with fragile white skin and big hazel eyes. She was carrying a baby in a sling. Just like me.

"Oh," she said, turning toward Elena, "Here she is! So alert! So well-formed!"

An explanation was given by Blake or the woman: they knew each other from Hopkins, and their son had been born just three weeks before Elena. We were all, it seemed, colleagues in this game of life.

"How are *you*?" she asked me as if we had known each other for years. She was readjusting the baby carrier, "My back is fucking killing me."

"We're okay," I fumbled. "Tell me it gets easier."

Blake took the baby from me and I returned my breast back inside the dress, moved in closer to see this woman's child. Blake was backing away towards the curb, the red-headed husband backing in the opposite direction, closer to the houses, I guess, nearer to his front door.

"You're breastfeeding?" asked the woman. "I've had mastitis. It's awful."

Then, just as I was about to break into conversation, another woman came by with a large dog and the babies started crying and the old hound howling and the woman said, "We should all get together."

"Yes," I offered. But Blake was head down, comforting Elena, walking quickly.

"She's Turkish," Blake said to me as we crossed over to our block.

"She's beautiful," I said.

But what I also meant was she's kind and so I was thrilled to see her again the next day.

I was alone, I mean with Elena, but not with Blake, and she was accompanied as before by her own baby, the red-headed husband and the hound, who seemed even more ancient than the day before. The husband stayed at a distance again and she came close to Elena who was in my arms.

"Blake's eyes?" she asked, as if I could also be responsible.

"I guess, but my father's were dark as well."

Elena started fussing as she often did those first months. I tried to think of something nice to say about their baby so I too went for eyes. How simple this all was: the solidarity amongst women, this sudden sharing, again the kindness.

"He looks just like you. His eyes."

"Really?" she laughed towards her husband. "Everyone says he looks like him."

Because her face was so open, I didn't want to be a bother and so I said something about having to keep going or Elena waking the dead.

"I'm so glad we got to meet her," the woman said, which seemed strange to me even then.

"Yes, nice to meet you too," I said and smiled at the husband.

Back at the house Blake was grading papers for his summer school students. His office was in the back bedroom and the window air conditioner made a suction sound that was calming for the baby. He was wearing pale blue boxer shorts and a white t-shirt; his hair was clumped with sweat.

"And so how was our walk, ladies?" he asked in his faux British accent.

"Good," I said. "Do you mind holding her? I might try for a shower."

Blake reached for Elena.

"I saw your friend, the Turkish woman," I called from the bathroom. "I want to make friends with them. I need some friends, Blake."

The cold water felt heavenly. Eight weeks on and I was coming back to life.

Blake was in the doorway, cradling Elena, glancing over his reading glasses. I pulled the curtain back a bit, "We could have them over for dinner, eat out back."

"Irene, she can't be your friend."

"Why not?" I asked.

"Because we were," he shifted the baby in his arms, "involved for a while."

My legs went weak. I was, I realized, no longer postpartum, no longer safe amongst women, but once again in competition for male attention. My body, all of our bodies, already, so quickly at play again. Really the respite, that mutual kindness, had been brief. Any grace period was over.

The woman, her flat white moon face and intelligent eyes, shook me. Never before had I felt jealous around Blake. There had been his ex-wife Angela, perfect. And then there had been disaster. The death of a child. It hardly, *I* hardly, had to do with sex. My bond to Blake had always seemed inevitable, but this woman made it feel common, and easily shattered.

To Blake I didn't say a word about the thoughts swirling around my head those sleepless nights. He was so happy with Elena, with our cave of love and new potential. I realized watching him of course that he had done this before, had lived through Joseph's infancy, had been awed at it all: the pregnancy and birth and those first heady weeks, but still he didn't seem sad, but hopeful, grateful for this new chance.

I was thankful that he had told me that I couldn't be friends with the woman and her red-headed husband. It was the decent thing to do; tell me the truth, keep things clean and uncomplicated.

"I'd make friends with her anyway," my sister Roberta said. "You need people now. And it's so boring at the beginning."

But I knew very well that I shouldn't. I wondered about this involvement. About Blake's life before Angela, before Joseph. About how old Blake had been, about how old the woman was now. Older than me, much older. Close to forty perhaps, the way these female professors had to jump through so many hoops before tenure, before being able to breathe.

And I kept turning it over again and again, like a smooth stone in the palm of my hand, my issue with all of this. Why this woman made me feel weak, exposed. Why she provoked in me a tenderness.

Elena was napping one evening so Blake and I actually ate dinner together. Cold pizza at the kitchen table. Blake poured a bottle of beer into two small glasses.

"We're doing okay, don't you think?"

"We are," I said.

"Still feel like you need a friend?"

"I do," I said. "Too bad you slept with the other mother on the street."

And I think my husband blushed.

"We weren't together long. I met her mother, though. An old Turkish woman—she loved me."

I couldn't bear to hear any other details. Something about that intimacy—the mother—hurt me.

I saw her again a few mornings later. I was alone, carrying two takeout coffees, heading back toward the house, my twenty minutes up. She didn't recognize me at first, she was rocking the baby carriage back and forth, whistling.

I waved though and then insisted.

"Hi, you don't recognize me without my baby, I'm Blake's wife."

Her face hardened and then opened up, "Yes, how are you? My name is Nina, by the way."

"Irene."

Then to be friendly, I said yet again, "Do tell me it gets easier."

"I just *left* yesterday," she said. "Went to a hotel for three hours! Told him I'd be back eventually. I needed to write. Do you write too?"

When I walked into our house the coffees had spilled all over me and I wondered who the too referred to—which writer: Blake or Angela? But it was the name that had truly shaken me. Nina. A Russian diminutive, but easily pronounced in both Spanish and English so it had been on our list. At the top of our list. We had called Elena Nina all the way up until the third trimester, but then one day we had changed our minds, liked Elena, for my aunt in Monterrey, my father's only sister.

"More modern than Nina," Blake had said. "More fun."

I couldn't get his colleague's face out of my mind: an old face. A classic beauty. Torturous to me. Every time I saw her on the street the confidence I'd gained through motherhood came undone. Elena was perfect, but suddenly not enough. I wanted what it was Nina had, some knowledge of Blake. A full, solid piece of him.

When Elena was about five months, she got easier. I could carry her around town strapped to my chest. She would coo up at the trees, sometimes even sleep. Those days I shopped a lot, not for clothes or books or anything fun. No, I stayed within a few blocks of home, in case the baby started crying, and haunted the food stores: the Giant supermarket, the Whole Foods on Falls Rd, the smaller shops closer to us. I was obsessed with pricing, knew, for the first time in my life, the exact price of tomatoes, oranges, a quart of milk, the best organic eggs, cheapest baby wipes. I paced Walgreens looking for organic body washes that might make me feel beautiful or womanly again.

Once a week I went into a hippie shop called Milagros on Elm Street to get a licorice flavored tea. Since sleep, sex, and alcohol had been taken away from me, things like herbal tea began to matter a great deal. Also, I liked the woman who ran the place. She talked to me instead of just looking at me with pity. One afternoon as I left the shop, a couple, linked at the hip, waved.

"Elena," said the man, "Elena, right?"

I adjusted Elena's hood, so the admirer could see her more clearly.

It was Nina's husband, but he looked younger, even handsome without the baby in tow.

"You're liberated," I said.

Nina's hair was down, I'd always seen it pulled back, always seen her tired like me.

Now I realized just how pretty she was, how happy they were.

"Leo's at the daycare," she said. "We're trying it out."

Then she looked at Elena and said, "She's such a combination of you two. Truly."

Years later I pass Nina sometimes on the way home from my daughters' school. We're both skinny, probably thinner than we've ever been in our adult lives. Bone tired, I overheard her tell someone on the phone once. We acknowledge each other once in a while. A nod, a wave. Today I was weak and gave a full-on broad open smile. I've never seen her son as a walking, talking child. The father must deal with him. Maybe he goes to private school or the art magnet. Our lives are no longer known to each other, there's no chance of conversation, no longer a tenderness, a vast distance now. Still, seeing her startles me every time: the realization that Elena could have been Nina, that Blake and any other woman could have had a child, that we're all so close to some other combination.

"It's silly," Blake tells us, "to ever calculate risk."

Close to dusk now, the light shifting in the safety of the kitchen. Our girls are doing word problems, solving for x and y.

Beatlemania

Craig Cotter

Paul McCartney called when I was cooking,
and was very coy and didn't have much to say.
This was mildly annoying
as I was concentrating on the five dishes I was preparing.

You in Scotland? I asked.

No, he said quietly.

Los Angeles?

No, he said distantly.

OK mate well I gotta run I'm cooking,
and I hung up.

Someone in my family
was tapping my phone,
and overheard McCartney being rude.

One of our family enforcers kidnapped Paul
and dropped him in a desert.
He was left with only the clothes he was wearing upon capture,
and our friend took everything out of his pockets.

Our friend monitored Paul wandering the desert with a drone at 30,000 feet.

By day two Paul—now 70—was severely sunburned and disoriented.
Our friend took a helicopter to meet him
with a full medical team.
Paul was treated and quickly recovered.

He was brought to my uncle's home in Las Vegas.

So you see, Paul, my uncle said, we both use the same guy.

Here's the deal—Craig's a big fan.
Don't call him and act like a dick.

Soap and Bones

Jerm Curtin

Her uncle could not bear the smell of soap
and bones – a side effect of Buchenwald –
so as a child, she had assumed
that he survived by virtue of his nausea.

I've never heard her speak of him till now.
She is intense, excited, and compares
the star-shaped leaves that fall from urban trees –
beautiful, yellow leaves – to the lives of lost

Jews. She picks one leaf, as if to check
there was no name or number graven on the back.
She's carried away, I know, by thoughts
of her own fragile self, of both of us,

suffering only by proxy. And by the thought
of streets, perhaps, now hidden under drifts
of yellow leaves, and of the trees that line
such idle streets, and shade the empty benches,

and of the shadows of the trees that fall
like sundials on the stained white-washed walls,
and of the peace, perhaps, in which
you no longer imagine growing old.

The Goblin of Tara

Patrick Deeley

You are skinny, drain-piped, high-booted,
your garish harp slung sideways
on a woollen *crios*, all but interchangeable
with your pelvis. Your fingernails
ping those strings, flaring them so everyone
at the banquet – even the high king –

falls into a swoon, yet listens again,
listens better, abandoned to the wild notes
you raise, whereupon you puff
flames, fan them with your swirling cloak.
Samhain after Samhain, you burn
the house down – hot licks, hit parade,

the halls of Tara blackened,
crumbling. And then you hightail it home
to your mounded fortress. Until
hard-headed Fionn, magicked against
your persuasive melodies, ends your life
and turns you into a legend.

Are you the first recorded pyromaniac?
Or even the first rock star? With
or without you, down the echo chamber
of ages, music carries rapture.
So it happens that a small boy, famished
for some sweetness in life,

finds it, or the promise of it, enchantment
an air which he must lean towards,
chirp of cricket, honk of wild goose,
or that resonance when a big wind clangs
the gate or sets the chimney
fluting. Soon, other music stirs this boy,

growing more abundant and diverse
as he grows: Joe Burke's *May Morning Dew*,
Vincent Broderick's *The Crock of Gold*,
Elizabeth Crotty groaning the box,
Leo Rowsome "pipering", Led Zep,
Bessie Smith, Ma Rainey, Mahalia Jackson,

Van Morrison. And the life of freedom
he craves sends him step-changing
to a disco jive, a funk rhythm.
Until he stands in a grassy amphitheatre,
chanting with the throng. A magenta sun
slips behind trees. Arc lights crawl

along cracked castle ramparts, making them
look reptilian. A dark royal river
rolling behind everyone and everything
plays at being motionless. Then
out you come – goblin again – swept
on a musical escalator through engines

of thunderbolt and smoke, with now
a squawking guitar mangled in your hands,
now a keyboard joy-jumping
about your knees, now a harpoon dragged
across your face, and you bless,
bless, at large in your latest incarnation.

Silence is better than poor grammar

Anne Freier

My ego is badland panting for answers
He roasts retort under our private stars

I count sheep their baa a hopeful choir
That I shall decode our quietus

By morning he's rubbed rockwool on his larynx
Grinds my questions into figments

From which I sample his apologies
The tenor of a phantom Will you speak?

But in the evening he cements his tongue
Coughs for lack of ventilation

I lick the dust from his lips
For a taste of translation

I Won't Call You Deathbell

Jake M.M. Griffin

Whichever side of the solstice I camped
I could not dampen my briared lamp out
Knotted in the brambled brush of hawthorn
Plotting a dull dusk most weary with doubt

Trust was dangled on a thin strand of silk
Hung on the barb of soft conversation
Baited with the honeyed tongue set dancing
Reeling home the sickest, sweet sensation

Foxglove tea held, no milk of the poppy
To pass easy into an unknown sleep

Rue it all, retching and clawing
Reaching into myself
Rome fell in an hour

But I won't call you deathbell, darling.

Three Poems
David Harsent

Shadow

His standing shadow, cast the length of the grave –
better this fine pretence than dance
on that ragged patch of meadowsweet and vetch.

Shadowfall on a grave: what to make of it? His voice
wrong in that field of stone, his shadow a misfit.
He holds up under a drench of birdsong.

His shadow darkens the grave: a tremor
of recognition, same shape and size, spit-
and-image it was said, something about the eyes.

A shadow bled over a grave goes face to face.
This portal, this empty stage. The farce of kinship.
As shame is a deepening stain, as grief is a cage.

Bone

She took a brush to what there was left of the skull.
Six women there were, each at work on a bone.
A hush fell on them as the thing came clear.

What there was left lay safe in the cup of her hand.
Nothing as planned. An eye-socket emptied of soil.
That wide smile given back; that gentle lie.

The way it came to hand, the way her brush
broke back the spoil, the way she lifted it
as if to speak, as if to ask a name.

Six women bringing the thing to light entire;
one palming the skull, waiting to hear it sing
what sorrows it owns, what weight of love, what blame.

Dreamstock

She dreamed his death each night; each night she came
to that same room and spoke his name; same room, same
white walls, white bed, lamp trimmed to shadowlight.

She dreams him dead. As before, that room; his name
spoken, as before. She goes in to him and it seems right.
His name comes back at her, deep-throated, broken.

She dreams him dead, near-dead, a sudden shift
locked-off in dream-time, framed in white and white
the backdrop. She dreamed again of what it kept or lacked.

Dreams of the dead: she arrives in person to watch
the past remake. In her waking version of this
she lies with him to find herself in the dim reach of his eyes.

Generational

Paul Ilechko

He is an old man now   but he was a big man
once   when it mattered   almost as broad
as he was tall   he was a working man and he
dressed the part   by which I mean he wore
a suit and a tie on the rare occasions he could
take his girl out for a treat   because such men
who were filthy all day long would need to look
good and smell good when the chance arose
even if the bruises on his hands would still
give him away   he believed in all things imperial
and the divine rights of kings   he believed
that the flooding rivers that burst their banks
from the storms of the excesses of capitalism
would somehow fail to wash away the little
that he owned   and by the time he awakened
from a dream turned nightmare   it was
too late to pause the rumbling carnage of
history   it was too late to save his generational
fantasies from crumbling into the cheap red
dirt of a trailer park   where his children
had no choice other than to throw their own
bodies at the same machine that crushed him
and the sound of their broken voices are
still echoing in his ears   overcoming even
the deafness of an old man   and the painful
memory   of the blindness that scarred his youth.

In the Summer of '76

Noel King

My piano teacher is playing catch-up term
this summer, having had her baby son;
the whirr of a fan interferes with the metronome.

We rinse our lettuce
under the slightest trickle
due to dreadful drought.

The man on the news says,
let the gardens die;
to keep water in the human taps.

My cousin presents me with warped
French chocolate from her school tour,
it melted and hardened, melted and hardened again.

The song of the summer is Silly Love Songs (Paul Mc Cartney)
I get that he used be a Beatle, my cousin educates me
on The Beatles, plays me his cassette of Sgt Pepper.

My Gran says she can smell
the burn of aviation fuel
from the jets that take-sky over her farm.

The bully-boy won't be in class in September,
I overhear his Dad tell my Dad they're moving to Carlow
as he hands over the cash for spuds.

In the haggard by our house
raising tomatoes, my father says,
has never been better.

My father is beaming, photographs everything
and everyone, rolls of film pile, awaiting development.
I am only eleven, will never be this happy again.

My Bespoke Life

Monique Debruxelles
Translated from the French by Laura Nagle

I was born in satin, silk, and percale. It was a Tuesday, and on Tuesdays my mother went to the fabric store to feed her obsession with sewing. The owner was an older gentleman with arms as long as a bishop's homily and the cheerful mien of a driver hopping into the sulky for the Prix d'Amérique. Her water broke as she walked into the shop. In the time it took her to pick out a new tape measure, some nylon thread, and a bundle of remnants, out I came, a screaming bundle of a different sort, eager to stitch together the fabric of my life.

My mother, already blessed with eight children, hadn't realized she was pregnant again. And in any case, it had to have come as a shock, given that my father, Joseph, had left her five years earlier, when Germaine was born. He was fed up, he'd said, as he stuffed everything within arm's reach into a suitcase. He'd had enough of providing for all these kids, each one uglier than the last and all of them of well below-average intelligence.

Granted, Germaine was born with a slightly dented head. She looked like something you'd see in a funhouse mirror. On the other hand, she was in all likelihood no dumber than most, but since she spent more hours asleep than awake, it was hard to be sure.

Romuald, seven years her senior, could have passed for an intelligent boy if only he'd have stopped walking around on his hands. Our mother said he'd been doing that ever since the day our father called him "an untrained monkey."

Mariella, the eldest, considered rounded lips to be inelegant and had therefore banished all words containing the long o sound from her vocabulary. She wasn't always easy to understand. For example, she wouldn't say "no," so she'd say "decline" instead. She took an interest in zoology, then otolaryngology, but had to give them up because she couldn't say what she was studying.

All my siblings have passed away except Eulalie. At age eighty-eight, she recently started law school so she can defend the recently apprehended man who attacked her in 1960. Is that a sign of intelligence? Our father would likely have seen it as yet more evidence of idiocy.

But here I've gone on at length about my family, when I'd planned to talk about something else entirely.

I had something of a tumultuous youth, but I came to realize it was time to settle down and stitch some quieter moments into the multicolored cotton knit of my days.

I was thirty years old, and I'd been seeing someone for a few months—the kind of guy who follows you around with sad puppy-dog eyes, and you let him, but only because you haven't found anyone better. Justin lived in a four-story downtown mansion stuffed to the rafters with art. He had so much of the stuff that he'd occasionally hide some items in the attic long enough to let them fade from memory, then take them out again and rejoice over them. The place looked like a museum, with items on display on every floor. Over time, his ancestors had gathered some very valuable works of art. In particular, his great-great-grandmother—"The Late, Great Adeline," Justin called her—had returned from her distant travels with paintings, sculptures, household items, and exquisite jewelry, some of it very old.

Every time I visited, my suitor would show me a few artworks he thought I'd surely enjoy, but they always left me cold. I couldn't understand how he could live with all that old crap lying around. But one day he showed me a little painting he'd found at the back of a closet, and it gave me a whole new perspective. It depicted the Virgin Mary, wearing an iridescent dress, changing the Baby Jesus's diaper as he lay amid an abundance of silk and satin. Such a nice, chubby baby, too. Pink as a pig's snout. I'd seen my fair share of representations of the Virgin Mary, but never was she engaged in a task like this. It was moving; it humanized her. Holy Mary, Changer of Diapers, had soft features, but this was not your typically bland, mawkish depiction. She was wiping her baby's bottom but looked as if her mind were elsewhere, perhaps stunned by this unlonged-for gift. And as for the half-naked little fellow eyeing the spectator—well, he looked ready to take a bite out of life. I was drawn to Mary and her baby boy, the two of them draped in soft, delicate silk. And I can't explain it, but I just knew somehow that they liked me too, that they wanted to shield me from harm.

After I left Justin's house that night, and even in the days that followed, I could feel them with me in spirit. It was like I was spellbound: I couldn't bear to spend another day without that painting. I needed it near me; I needed to have it within sight. I tried to get Justin to sell it to me. I didn't care if it meant incurring a debt my grandchildren would still be paying off decades later. But he just laughed at me. "Acquiring a work of art is like adopting a pet," he told me. "It's permanent. You give them their forever home." But he thought up another solution: If I married him, I could admire the painting every day, to my heart's content.

At first I dismissed his proposal. I thought it would be preferable to have someone—a person with certain skills—steal the painting for me. But I didn't know where to turn for that sort of thing. I spent days looking into it, to no avail. So I reluctantly agreed to be joined with him in matrimony. Justin howled with joy, kissed my hands and forehead, and hugged me so tight that I could feel the golden thimble I'd inadvertently swallowed at age fifteen coming dislodged deep in my innards. When my fiancé finally let me go and I got a chance to catch my breath, the buck's head mounted over the fireplace was looking down at me with contempt.

We set a date for our wedding. And that's when my troubles began.

Justin's family was no less complicated than mine. While he had no living parents or siblings, he was positively dripping with uncles, aunts, and more or less distant cousins, plus a great-grandmother whose company was about as enjoyable as that of a rabid hyena. But Justin adored her and visited her several times a week. Even though she was ninety-eight and had irreversible vision problems, she still drove around in a flaming red Triumph convertible wearing a Formula I helmet, with a cigar hanging out of her mouth and a basset hound by her side. When Justin introduced me to his great-grandmother, she and her dog looked me up and down, and finally the old lady sighed, "Do as you please, darling boy." The basset hound said nothing, but it was clear enough he shared her opinion.

Uncle Honoré, whose crooked mouth reminded me of a poorly sewn buttonhole, was more enthusiastic. So enthusiastic, in fact, that Justin had to fight him off me with a well-placed uppercut. Alas, that was the end of the road for my raw silk skirt.

Aunt Léonie and her son Éloi were hardly moved by the announcement of our engagement; all they wanted to know was what we'd be serving at the reception. I eat like a bird, so I didn't much care. But it mattered greatly to Léonie and Éloi, who had voracious appetites and followed a strictly anthropophagous diet; for them, eating anything other than human flesh was out of the question. I listened to them debate the respective nutritional value of young Boro girls' toes versus Fulani soldiers' kidneys for three hours straight.

"Are we absolutely obligated to invite them?" I asked Justin as we left their house.

"Of course, sweetheart. We're a very tight-knit family. You'll get used to it soon, you'll see."

I had my doubts.

Meanwhile, cousin Jean-Marc, who had served twelve years in prison for pedophilia, insisted on warning me that Justin was a pervert and was just hiding his predilections well. "He'll make you miserable, you poor dear! You'd better cut and run before it's too late." My fiancé got a good laugh out of that joke and amiably retaliated by twisting Jean-Marc's arm behind his back. We dropped him off at the nearest emergency room on our way home.

Of cousin Charles and Aunt Gracieuse, all I'll say is that their lifestyle utterly depressed me.

Two hundred eighty people in all were invited to our wedding. "It'll be nice and cozy," said Justin, who thankfully didn't have many friends. For my part, I didn't want any of my family there, and I was far too ashamed of my choice to invite my friends.

I knew full well I was making a mistake, but I went ahead with the wedding because *Virgin Changing a Diaper* had become indispensable to me. Justin clung to me like Velcro, but on the rare occasions he gave me a bit of freedom, I ventured into seamy bars in hopes of encountering a skilled thief. That's how I met the artist Césarine V. She spent her days with a little notebook, sketching the faces of the people she encountered. She was a slender young woman, cool as linen, who radiated confidence. I observed her for a while as she sketched an old man playing cards, capturing his menacing expression and the gunk in his eyes. She was so focused on her task that it took her a while to notice I was watching. She looked up at me, briefly startled. Then she scrutinized my face, shamelessly sizing me up. I went over to her table and asked, "Do I remind you of someone?"

By way of response, she stood and led me over to a mirror hanging near the counter. It was no wonder she was stunned: Looking at us side by side, we could have been twins. Our hair was different, but other than that, the resemblance was uncanny: same silhouette, same height, same features. Right away I realized how I could use this to my advantage. A plan took shape in my mind. Césarine, posing as me, would get Justin out of the house, giving me an unassailable alibi so I could steal *Virgin Changing a Diaper*. Then I'd skip town. And if Césarine took a shine to my fiancé, he was all hers; she was welcome to marry him in my place. With just three days to go before my fateful walk down the aisle, I had no choice but to place my trust in my doppelgänger. I laid out the situation for her. She couldn't help but be swept up in the scheme; I suppose she had the fanciful nature so common in artists. And it probably didn't hurt that I wrote her a fat check on the spot.

And so it was that she rang Justin's doorbell the very next day, sporting a fresh haircut and one of my suits, while I observed from behind the wheel of a rental car. To keep from being recognized, I was wearing a brown wig, thick-framed round eyeglasses, and old clothes belonging to one of my sisters.

My fiancé opened the door for her.

"Sweetheart! Don't you have your keys?"

"No, I think I've lost them."

The door closed on them. A good hour or so went by. While waiting, I watched the people in the street. I imagined what they might be doing or thinking, where they were headed. A young girl skipped along, practically dancing down the sidewalk. Perhaps she'd just managed to convince her parents to let her go to the dance. And that fellow who looked like a hidalgo, carrying a rectangular package under his arm—I figured him for a frame-maker. His self-satisfied pout suggested he was on his way to meet a client who was sure to be pleased with his services and would undoubtedly reward him with more work.

The cassock-clad priest skimming the walls and nearly breaking into a run didn't stimulate my imagination at all.

Just when I was starting to get bored and wonder what Césarine and my fiancé were up to, they came down the front steps, hand in hand, beaming. I waited for five minutes, watching them disappear into the distance. Then I strolled as casually as possible up the steps, hoping there weren't any busybodies peering through the neighbors' windows. I took the keys from my pocket and quickly slipped into the house.

Virgin Changing a Diaper was kept on the third floor, in a small sitting room with gray wallpaper, facing the gable. I climbed up. The spot over the console table, where the painting was normally on display, was empty. I looked all around. Where the hell had Justin put it? I went across the hall into his bedroom: nothing. I scoured all the other rooms on the third floor, then the fourth, then the first. The *Virgin* was nowhere to be found. I checked my watch. Césarine was free for just two hours that afternoon. She'd been very clear with me that she couldn't offer me any more time. She was to visit the great-grandmother, then part ways with Justin downtown, claiming she had a dress fitting appointment, and promise to catch up with him that evening. Knowing my fiancé to be a homebody, I was sure he'd be back any minute. I reluctantly left empty-handed, leaving the front door open. The plan I'd flimsily stitched together called for Justin to be tricked into thinking he'd forgotten to lock it. It didn't even occur to me to question whether there was any point in following the plan anymore.

Then I went to my dress fitting, but I forgot to run home and change first. It took the good woman a moment to recognize me, at which point she gave me a weird look. I offered a lavishly embroidered excuse for my apparel and gave her my wig for her grandkids to play with.

I returned to my fiancé's house around seven, taking the road that ran along the gable side of the house. The clouds suddenly parted in my mind, and I realized what had happened: Césarine had stolen *Virgin Changing a Diaper*. She'd distracted Justin, gone up to the gray sitting room, and thrown the painting out the window into the waiting arms of her accomplice—the man I'd taken for a framer. The simplest of plans! I was sure Césarine would soon be in touch to give me the painting. Not wanting to miss her when she called, I decided to cut short my evening with Justin. He was totally discombobulated, the poor dear.

"A painting of mine was stolen," he'd said by way of greeting. "Your favorite, *Virgin Changing a Diaper*. When we left the house, I forgot to lock the door. I guess your enthusiasm really wore me out earlier this afternoon, and I just wasn't thinking straight. When I came home, the front door was ajar. I didn't much worry about it, since everything was in order on the first floor. But I was going to wrap the *Virgin* in a nice box, as a gift for you on our wedding night. I went up to the third floor and it was gone."

I mulled over this revelation, the threads of my sanity unraveling.

"Nothing else was taken?"

"Yes, actually. The thief also stole our wedding rings from the drawer in my nightstand—where I put them this afternoon after I'd shown them to you. But don't worry, darling. I'll buy us new rings tomorrow. Our wedding will go forward as planned."

Césarine didn't bring me the painting that evening, nor the following day. The day after that, I ran over to the bistro where we'd met. No one there had seen her recently or knew where she lived. All at once my obliviousness was torn to shreds like the lining of an old coat. The scoundrel had put one over on me.

And so the wedding went on as planned, with Justin's two hundred eighty guests and all my relatives to boot. I don't know who told them. They showed up in the middle of the ceremony: Germaine with her pillow; Romuald walking on his hands; Mariella, who was in the process of eliminating the *u* sound in addition to the *o*; and all the rest of them, with my mother and her crafting tote bringing up the rear. Justin was a perfect gentleman. He formally invited them to the reception, but I could tell from his chilly attitude that he'd have called the whole thing off if he'd met them earlier.

My marriage wasn't as unhappy as I'd feared, although I did nearly die of boredom on numerous occasions. We had five lovely children, who left us, one after the other, as soon as they reached legal age. We never heard from any of them again. Whatever became of Gladys, who used to recite poetry while plucking the hairs off her arms, one by one, with a pair of gherkin tongs? Or Jean-Robert, long known as Marinette (hey, we all make mistakes)? Or Hugues, with his shark-like skin and webbed feet, who refused to learn how to swim? Or the conjoined twins, whose names I've forgotten? Children are so ungrateful.

Despite these annoyances, my life was close to happy. The only thing I really missed was the benevolent gaze of the *Virgin Changing a Diaper*. I dreamed once of hiring a private investigator to track down Césarine V., but what would be the point? Surely she'd have gotten rid of the loot as soon as she could.

For our seventh wedding anniversary, Justin gave me a painting. He used to visit all the galleries, never missed an opening, and knew lots of artists.

"This is the work of a young painter, a lady who looks an awful lot like you, as it happens. Her name is Césarine V. It's uncanny, really; I nearly mistook her for you. When I saw this painting, I was immediately taken with it. I hope you'll love it just as much."

I hid my astonishment and opened my present. It was the complete opposite of *Virgin Changing a Diaper*. An ungainly woman dressed in red and yellow gazed obsessively at the baby playing at her feet, as if nothing else existed. The child, who was giving the viewer a look as pointed as a needle, had the features of a grumpy old man. I couldn't fathom why my husband was so fond of a painting that treated such a mundane subject in such a monumentally ordinary way. The colors were garish, the characters ugly and unpleasant. Standing before this vision of oppressive maternal love, I felt like a third wheel.

"I had a long conversation with Césarine V.," Justin said. "I told her all about you, what your taste is like. This painting wasn't for sale, but she was certain you'd like it and insisted that I give it to you. She said it couldn't be in better hands."

I'm not the type to accept any old gift just because it's supposedly the thought that counts. That gift was uniquely repulsive to me, and I would cheerfully have kicked it to the curb if it weren't for the fact that I was looking to make amends for something at the time. No big deal; a trifle, really. It just wasn't the right moment to be ungracious. Always best to mend a tear before it gets any bigger. So I sucked it up and thanked Justin effusively for his gift. He put it on display in the dining room, where for years I took my meals with that nauseating scene in my face.

***

My husband died. I saw him to his final resting place without inordinate sadness, though I did feel I'd miss him. He bequeathed me usufruct of his entire fortune, but at my age, it's hard to enjoy it. The skein of my lifetime unfurled at the same pace as his; I have only a few meters of thread left.

Last week I took Césarine's atrocious painting down from the wall and threw it into the fireplace, with the buck looking on cynically. I suppose I could have sold it, but I don't need the money, and the thought of someone taking joy from that painting sent shivers down my spine. And so the painting burned, to my great relief.

The next day, a letter came for me in the mail, signed Césarine V. "I know death is near, but before I go, I must explain to you why I did what I did. When you suggested I should help you steal *Virgin Changing a Diaper,* I found it amusing to pull the rug out from under you. It was so simple that I took the rings, too, just to spice things up. I was planning to have them returned to you at the wedding; I'm an honest person by nature. But I was desperately in need of money at the time. I used to draw the clientele at some bistros, as you know, and you meet the strangest people that way. A regular at the Bijou Bar gave me a nice chunk of change for your rings. Be grateful, because if I hadn't taken them, maybe I would have sold the *Virgin* instead. But I wouldn't have gotten as much for it. You know nothing about art. Sure, the subject is kind of unusual, but the painting isn't worth much, even given its age. I kept it, figuring I'd give it back to you someday. But I just couldn't stand looking at the Blessed Virgin's punchable face. I painted a different scene of motherhood over it. I got a number of offers for that painting, but I always refused to sell it. And then one day, your husband came and visited my studio. (That dear man! I was sad to read in the newspaper that he died. So kind, so astute, so passionate about art. I hope you made him happy?) I practically forced him to buy that painting for you. Without realizing it, you've been admiring your *Virgin Changing a Diaper* day after day for all these years..."

I didn't finish reading the letter. I tore it up and threw it in the trash. Since then I've spent hours sitting by my cold hearth, where a few ashes remain.

The original story "La vie cousue main" appeared in Monique Debruxelles' book *Croisés chez Kordilès* (Éditions Rue des Promenades, 2013).

Athos in August

Ian Fisher

ELYSIUM, 12 August 2020—When I arrived last week, the first thing I asked about was restaurants. Because of the virus, I hadn't eaten out in five months. No problem, they said, our restaurants are all open and we know the kind you like.

They explained to me metamorphosis: that my appearance would be optimized seamlessly to reflect an appropriate age for my changing circumstances. Then, I filled out all their forms with a Montblanc Fountain Pen (Writers Edition Homage to Victor Hugo), which they said I could keep. The fountain pen was silver and black; the ink was peacock blue.

On that first night, I took the Q-train over to Junior's where I was seated right away.

I'll have a Reuben, I said.

Sorry, the menu is vegetarian, said the waitress, who reminded me of the winsome waif Audrey Tautou in the film *Amélie.*

You're kidding, right? I said, looking around the place. The superannuated customers were dining on chopped eggplant and Tam Tams. *Latkes* with applesauce. *Kasha* and bowties. Borscht. Compôte. They were drinking Dr. Brown's Original Cream Soda.

No, *ma parole d'honneur,* she said. Up here you've got to keep going forever. No meat on the menu.

So what you're telling me, then, is that it's the exact opposite of what Richard Goodwin says in *Quiz Show*?

I don't know: I haven't seen that one.

Goodwin, a Jew, is having lunch at a private club. And he says to Van Doren, "They have the sandwich here, but they don't seem to have any Reubens."

You know, the waitress said, they warned me about you. That you were *un blagueur,* a joker. Now what will you have to eat, honey?

Lyonnaise potatoes and some *cole*slaw, I said. Lyonnaise potatoes and some *cole*slaw.

After a cup of joe and a slice of strawberry cheesecake with graham crust topped with macaroon crunch, I walked south along Flatbush Avenue. I wanted to retrace the after-school paper route I had as a kid. It was a sultry Spaldeen summer evening with a slight breeze, perfumed as if by heather, blowing from the harbor. A few stars glimmered.

I was once again Charles Baudelaire's *flâneur*—a passionate city spectator who rejoices in his incognito—passing the homes, schools, playgrounds, shops, bars and restaurants, and churches and synagogues of the hamlets of Brooklyn.

The streets were almost deserted of pedestrians. Sporadic sounds wafted from apartment windows. Not conversations or music or television: it was a baseball game on kitchen radios. I couldn't make out the words, but the pitch and rhythm of the announcer's voice were familiar. At Grand Army Plaza, I decided to veer left instead of right, around the top of Prospect Park.

As I got closer to Washington Avenue and Sullivan Place, I heard an explosive roar from a crowd. Before I even saw it, I knew this was Ebbets Field and the Dodgers were playing under the lights. I recalled my friend Frankie Bertinelli's telling me, years ago, that the real year began not on January first but on the day Red Barber started broadcasting from spring training.

I walked over to a turnstile guard. Who's in town? I said.

You ain't a fan, are you? he said.

Yeah, since before you were born, I said.

Well, then, you musta just got into town: we play the same game heeah ev'ry night.

What game is that?

Tuesday, October 4, 1955.

But *that* game, you know, was played in the Bronx.

Youz in Hamill Heaven, now, fella: we moved that game ovah to Ebbets.

What inning are they in?

Bottom of the sixth.

So it's 2-0 already?

Hey, you really *are* a fan.

Yeah. Has Berra batted yet?

Not yet.

Can I get in?

Sure.

But I don't have any cash on me.

This game's fohr free, fella. Come on in.

Although my feet wanted to take me to the outfield bleachers, I somehow found the press box. Nobody asked me for credentials, nobody hassled me. At the center of the row, I spied a familiar figure hunched over an Underwood typewriter, punching the keys: *pa-papa-pa-pap-pa-papa-papa-pa-pap.*

In a former life, this man—who singlehandedly reinvented the newspaper column—was described as a bowling ball fuelled with liquid oxygen. We had worked together once, across the hall from each other. They called us 'the princes of print'. But how any person with normal eyesight could have mistaken me for him was still a mystery to me.

What are *you* doing here, Jimmy? I said. You're a Mets lover.

Sin*ah*trah sent me ovah the Bridge; he's waitn' fohr you at Jilly's. He heard you were in town, and he sent me to get you.

Come on, Jimmy. Let me at least see Sandy's one-hander and throw to Pee—

Nah, Pete, we can't keep him waitn'. You know how he is. You can watch this game ev'ry night from tomorrah until eternity. You can watch Gil Hodges and Johnny Podres perfohrm their magic. No Jackie *Robb*insin, though. It's his Achilles heel, or his knees, or some other pain that jumped all the way from *Robb*insin's body into the manager's cranium.

I sure would like to see Robinson again. He's the Holy Ghost, you know?

Sure. Branch Rickey's bringn' *Robb*insin into the majohs changed forevah not only baseball, but the country, and evenchully the entiyah wohrld; it was the lawhjist single act of ouwhah time. Ask Sin*ah*trah to take you up to Yankee Stadium. They play Larsen's perfect game *thehr*. But you'll have to suffah through Mantle's homah off Maglie, and his catch off Hodges.

Sinatra's not a Yankees fan, Jimmy.

Well, I guess he likes them playin' that song of his—*New Yauwk, New Yauwk*—ev'ry night. Anyway, let's stop lollygaggin' and get goin'. Sin*ah*trah's bin waitn' fohr you fohr ovah twenty yeeahs.

Jimmy, you do know that I don't drink anymore.

That's okay, Sin*ah*trah'll drink enuf fohr the both of you. He's back with Ava now, and she's drinkn' too. She remembahs meetn' you once, aftah the divohrce, at his place at the *Wahl*dohrf, and she wants to apologize to you. Somethin' about her whackn' a small dog with a tabloid. Martin and Lewis are up theh: they've kissed and made up too. Jackie O, Susan Sontag, and Nora Ephron. John Lennon and Gene Krupa. Seamus Heaney and Joe Liebling. Even Bobby Kennedy said he might drop by. It's, auhh, sort ova welcome-home pahrty fohr you.

Sinatra and Kennedy are like beer and milk, I said. *Not at all a good mixture.* Those two wouldn't be seen dead in the same saloon.

I brokered a peace treaty fohr tonight's shindig. Like between the Protestants and the Catholics. Or between the Muslims and the Jews. I told 'em, auhh, let bygones be bygones: the Poet Lawhreate of Pawhrk Slope has finally come home.

It was as simple as that, was it?

Bee-*yoou*tihful, Jimmy said.

I wanted to ride the train—and stand in the first car like I used to with my kid brother Tommy, watching the station lights race towards us through the tunnel and gleaning the exotic languages of people of all ages from all over the world—but Jimmy had a Checker Cab waiting for us. Going over New York, I asked what he thought about the recent HBO documentary about us.

Nevvah sawhr it, he said.

I told him about COVID-19 and its devastating toll upon the city we both loved more than any other.

Dies *this* city, dies the wohrld, he said.

The drive was about forty-five minutes north: Flatbush Avenue to the Brooklyn Bridge to the FDR Drive, Exit 9 for East 42nd Street. We turned right onto Eighth Avenue and then right again onto West 52nd Street. Stretch limousines lined the block.

When the Checker pulled up to Jilly's, I reached for my wallet: I'd forgotten it wasn't there. I don't have any cash on me, Jimmy, I said.

Fohrgettaboutit, he said. Your money's no good up heeah.

Even before we were waived through, I could hear Kirsty MacColl singing, from beyond the red velvet rope border of the bar, *Fairytale of New York*. About New York's being *no place for the old*. I disagreed with her, of course, but then again I wasn't old anymore.

Jimmy recognized one of the wiseguys who couldn't shoot straight, loitering at the long mahogany purgatory, and strolled over to chat. I continued past the cordon into the back room. Sinatra's friend Jilly Rizzo—who, thanks to Sinatra, played bit rôles in *The Manchurian Candidate, Tony Rome,* and *The Detective*—shook my hand.

'Ey, Petey babe, he said, his bad eye glinting. It's been a long time.

Yeah, I said. Yeah, decades.

Hey, stranger in the night, did you eat yet? It was Sinatra, seated in a leatherette booth against the wall, summoning me. He was pointing at me like I was Walt Frazier and had just assisted him on an alley-oop in Madison Square Garden. A lit cigarette was resting against a black ashtray in front of him, next to a glass of what I guessed was a mix of two fingers of Jack Daniel's whiskey, a splash of water, and four ice cubes. I walked over and stared down at his scarred face, into those legendary bright blue eyes. He was smiling that boyish smile of his. He stood up—I was always surprised by how short he was—and we hugged.

The reunion of *High School Dropout Survivors Anonymous,* I said.

Grab a seat, Sinatra said, sliding a blue bottle of Brooklyn Seltzer Boys and a Baccarat crystal glass towards me. Ava, say hello to my Mick kid brother.

Welcome home, Mr. Hamill, she said. Frankie has been looking forward to this for a very long time. Have *you*?

I had met Ava Gardner once before, when she was in her fifties, drinking, and appearing in disaster films. Tonight, however, Ava was in her late twenties and impossibly beautiful. I could see what Sinatra saw in this *femme fatale,* and how their breakup had inspired his *In the Wee Small Hours* album.

You know, Ava, I said, I didn't realize it until just now but I *have* been looking forward to this, yeah. *Sláinte!*

Cent'Anni, said Sinatra, clinking his glass with mine. What are you recommending for reading these days, Peter? I still have trouble sleeping at night.

Fly Already, by Etgar Keret. He's a guy from Israel who's really got the gift for language, for the magic and jewelry of words, I said. *Madame Bovary* by Gustave Flaubert. *Don Quixote* by Cervantes. *On Old Age* by Cicero. You can never go wrong with the classics.

But if the book doesn't *speak* to you—if you don't *get* its writer—lay it aside.

Dyin' is one huge pain in the ass, ain't it? Sinatra said. But, for *us*, that's yesterday's news. There's about two dozen people here who want to talk to you.

Breslin told me Senator Kennedy might drop by, I said. I don't see him.

I told Jilly to disinvite him. Italians can hold grudges just as long as Irishmen.

And, according to Clyde Haberman, Jews, too, I said.

Talking about Jews, take a look over there, Sinatra said. He jerked his head to his right.

Seated at the next booth was Meyer Lansky, dragging on a Cohiba Behike 52. The last time I had seen him was in the forties, when he staged a daring Christmas Eve rescue for my friend Lev Augstein, a concentration camp survivor, from a children's shelter in Brooklyn.

Hey, sport, said Lansky. Welcome home. Lev told me to tell you it's like Christmas every day.

I laughed out loud. Meyer, what ever happened to Walter O'Malley? I said.

O'Malley's in a windowless basement studio apartment, said Lansky, the kind you find under the stoops of slum tenements. Rumor has it he's studying bugs.

Why *bugs*? I said.

The only person who talks to him is J. Edgar Hoover.

And then, as I was checking out the room through a purple haze of secondhand smoke, I locked eyes with a solitary woman staring at me. The first woman I ever loved: Annie Devlin, as was.

She had arrived in New York from Belfast the day of the 1929 stock market crash, and paid for the passage *ex post* by working several years as a maid for rich people. She had lived in a coal-stove-heated railroad flat with linoleum floors. Beginning in the mid-thirties, she filled Christmas stockings—which increased in number seven times—with tangerines and walnuts on credit from the neighborhood grocery store. Although a Catholic, she questioned God's motives for her family's poverty.

This was a woman who embraced education and intelligence. Before I could read, she read to me. The first book she read me was *The Story of Babar: The Little Elephant* by Jean de Brunhoff, the genesis of my gallomania. Later, she insisted that I have a library card, because the road out of poverty started, five hundred yards from my home, at the public library, that sanctuary of memory and wisdom. When I was eleven, I read in bed *The Three*

Musketeers by Alexandre Dumas—"All for one, one for all"—and imagined I was Athos. When I quit Jesuit high school and went to work at sixteen, this woman cried; I had never seen her cry before.

There was no person in that room—or, for that matter, anywhere else—I wanted to see or talk to more than her. I stood up from Sinatra's booth, and walked over to her, leaned over, and kissed her.

Oh, Peter, you're home, she said. You look great, lad. I ordered some Social Tea cookies and a cup of strong tea with milk and sugar for you.

Thanks, Mom, I said.

Have you honored our pain, Peter? she said.

I understood exactly what she meant. I was the first son of immigrants from the Old Country, like Sinatra was. People who had come so far and sacrificed so much in order that their children could have a better life in this country whose streets were paved in gold.

She had taught me about learning, hard work, and grace; she had taught me about the world in the *right* way. She taught me the meaning of two four-letter words that start with an *L* and end with an *E*: *Love* and *Life*.

I had loved family, and women, and friends; I had loved an entire city. And I had lived a life, not an apology. I had made something with my hands and fingers and heart: concrete nouns and active verbs. Like Sinatra had made something with his voice and *his* heart. Something that would last. Something that would be remembered long after we were gone.

Hey, Mom, I said, my book *Irrational Ravings* is selling for $967 on Amazon: how about *that!?*

Twitchy

Sandra Kolankiewicz

You can't remember who you are, sighs LiLi, *but*
maybe with the whiskey and the beatings you never

knew. I've heard all about her too, how there are war
zones & war zones. She provides no adjective for

their differentiation, how one has bullets, and in the
other a brother or sister can disappear, end up on a milk

carton, automatically aged by computer progression.
How there are drones & also drones, best if you marry

one, for that's the preferred kind of man, who doesn't
want to sting, no violence in his nature, just docile and

digging into a daisy swaying in the breeze, laden with
pollen. The other kind, the one that spies, should be

avoided. Both men and women have traced the scars
on her ear lobe, on her lip and neck, enquired what

happened. I've no need to touch them, have my own
to hide, reveal, have someone catch sight of without my

knowing, a glimpse into potential understanding that in a
small town turns to judgement, how there are stories &

stories, the ones you merely tell, the ones told, the ones
partially heard or totally misunderstood, the ones in which

you now play a part, shared every night around family tables
until the only souls who know themselves are those wrong

in their interpretation, who never noticed the bruises on
their own ribs, the discolorations seen as their shirt moves

when they bend over, who forgot there are both marks & marks,
used either to designate or grade. *You're twitchy,* she says.

Response to an alien cartography

Christopher Konrad

Crows sound the alarm at all times of day but it's those
held in conference of their murders that yield the
dark-sludge-certainty of earth's rattles: it is the corvine call
to arms for those dumb to the kraaaaarck call of black beasties who
point the way with ebony beaks shiny like armour and aimed like
truth-knives at those nested in the halls of cowardly power.

... thoughts seeded like grevillea birds swaddled in honey, drip drip
dripping like tumblers emptying into flensed ribcage of a contagion
reminiscent of plagues of past: skin slated with undecipherable
codes like bird-prints and beak marks scoring an opera open to a deep
deep night: stars dead yet shining like grinning million-year-old cadavers
which have watched over us for longer than we have been simian-sapiens.

Today the hrab watches like black feathered towers over our personal
declensions into a perfect maelstrom of purposelessness and idiot-repose.
How is it we cannot curse those leathery saurian breeds escaped from chthonic
ornithines of aeons past and which brought their dark speech into the world
of men: their aaarrrckk-squawks seam through the long millennia into the ears
of monkeys which then ape-mime into lungs, larynx slipped onto lips and
tongues and scrawled into stone become speech and word and script.

Anointy ointy pointy birds, descendants of beast of prey and here to entertain
dreary minds and make fools of us all. Crows look back at diminutive ancient
cousins and send out knives from dark bottomless eyes and little cousins fly
home to consider their chatty ways. I recognise no authority in this world
and those dark ancestor birds accompany me on that mongrel path.

The Stars

Anthony Lawrence

The jade bracelet Pontius Pilate wore
before a magus, masquerading as a money lender,
had hexed it into a marker for betrayal

and earmarked it for burial as a time capsule,
was stolen by someone whose name
was a portmanteau, often misheard as corrugation

and worn to a ball whose entry
required the wearing of a mask, in this case
a hybrid loon and egret affair, which gave the eyes

a haunted countenance, and because
everyone had sworn to withhold speech
and touch, those human needs interchangeable

as weeping and rain on the original sleep app:
the wind-assisted sweep of palm fronds
over stone, and used by those for whom

the words *circadian* and *rhythm* were all
they needed, they played Guess the Guest,
and practiced iridology by staring

without blinking like a mongoose into coded,
intimate dark, remembering that deep-sleep
breathing was only a sound or two removed

from silence, and even without pressing an ear
to the homespun weave a partner
in strangerhood was wearing, to hear her blood

or his oxygen, they were able to take
the scenic route around the electrified field
of a body, the bolted terrain God had mined

with stations for prayer and tripwires
for non-believing travellers, they breathed,
and were mindful of how prolonged exposure

to candleflame can capture rare seams of light
from spikes in solar activity. Now they had seen
the trailer, they could lie down with the stars.

July's Last Fever Dream

Mercedes Lawry

I have swallowed Kafka.
I have turned inside out,
pleading, at sunset, as a ghost
cloud reveals a softened moon.
I have given up logic,
swum upstream past the eerie ferns,
heard whispers of inverted language
and smashed the clocks.

I have not become a creature,
any creature, though I've tried,
wriggling arms and legs, snapping
at flies. The sag of the body.
I give up, it cries. How much water
is left – in the lake, in the cistern,
in the layers of sediment, trickling?

Let Sartre in too, but keep
his whining at a minimum. This here,
this nothing, is, was and will be.
Blessed sleep, I wait for you.
I've placed the ice on my heart.
It changes nothing. The day will finally
give up. Let's go, boys, I call, dreams await.

Paper Cranes in B-Flat Minor

Chin Li

I watched you and the wee one cross the border
into semi-safety, before going back to my dugout—
my awkward position on the dreaded frontline.
I drank my bitter coffee from my battered flask,
and imagined making paper cranes one after another
until I counted more than a thousand,
and then sent them all to you in my head
at the first note of the B-flat minor.
You'll remember the wee one had made
a paper crane for me before the two of you left:
it's now sleeping in my breast-pocket.
Should a bullet find my chest (it will, sooner or later),
this little crane will soothe me in death,
for I know your love lives in this origami badge.
I'll kiss it with my last breath, and let it fly,
let it fly away to your side. 'Love thy enemies'...
O how hard, how very hard! I felt sick when bombs
were dropped on us, bombs the Patriarch had blessed,
as if they were precious, divine gifts.
(*Does God not have eyes to see?*)
How I wish I could fold the world into a little paper crane,
and put it in my pocket for safekeeping.
It'll soon be snowing: Have you got something hot to drink?
Now my stiff fingers on the trigger, I'm ready—
But *them* on the other side, are they not sons and fathers?
Do they not also feel pain?
I know when the artillery rounds begin,
I'll start singing the song in B-flat minor,
that love-poem you've lovingly taught me to sing,
so if we have to travel through the land of the dead
(I will, but I hope you won't), we shan't ever forget.

Good Bodies

Elizabeth Loudon

The men have brought us a lamb entire,
bones for the breaking and a throat-shine of bleating

stunned for Greek Easter tenderness.
We watch them watching it drip on a spit,

our hair stirred by a hilltop breeze. A young wife
in skin-tight jeans comes forward to wipe a spill,

or a sister – nobody's asking, these are the men
who arrive in boats from Albania that land at night,

biding their time. When we talk of the heat
that never cools we are talking of mouths to feed

and others to starve, of babies that crawl
too near to the fire but are not our business.

Our host wears a cape and hangs his gun
on a wall so nobody gets ideas. He knows

how it all turns out, his body's an oracle,
and the men will outwait and outwit him

if he sleeps too well in his lonely estate.
Once a woman lived here who did for him

what the men now do, but he sent her
away and she fell from a temple ledge,

or she fell and he said that he sent her.
He says, *she had a good body*. We arrange

our faces in sorrow but he calls for more wine,
then reminds us who owns the vineyards and sheep.

The men who lean over our shoulders to serve us
are sober as mercenaries at dawn. He says,

she should have known better than to climb so high.

BIG LOVE

Michael Martin

Big love to all the astronauts, even the ones
that only went to the Space Station.
All best to a poignant postcard
lying across the car seat.
Hugs and kisses to pillows
taking the internet by storm!
A toast if you will to the young fellow
giving Abstract Art one last chance.
Big shout-out if you tried to love thy neighbor.
Thoughts and prayers to that weird way
a dead lightbulb feels inside your palm.
Salud to the Stalinists who didn't murder Dada.
Raise a glass to the squirrels
doing it doggy-style in the dog park,
and a big round of applause to the usher
pointing her pen light to an empty seat
and regards to the concussed snowflakes
that pelted the widow's window and stuck
around as long as they could before melting
into a wash of grief,
and now a moment of silence for the pet hamster
being passed between the children because
love is killing him too.

At the Call Centre

David McLoghlin

(November 2020 – February 2021)

The messy black Yaris still parked outside the abandoned unit.
Shrubs overtake video cameras, a chair buttresses a fire door
like a bulwark against zombies. Silence travels further
in the business park semi-*deserta,* along corridors of silver birch:
almost evocative of tree-tunnel secondary roads in the *Midi*
or the Spanish *Costa*—where we don't go, bands of paint
luminous on the holm oaks of the bypassed old main road.
An elderly dog-walker walks the circuit, car parks linked
like lagoons: her assigned daily escape from cocooning. And
it is pleasant in Bishopstown: to be onsite, taking a stroll
from the call centre outsourced to UK markets, discovering a path
in unpruned topiary, to another unit among trees.

Tunnels only open for children who meet the spirit of the forest
in the cartoon film my toddler watches. In a distance year
with no crèche, she knows the "two 'lil gurls" better than friends,
though sometimes still mentions Sepo, Eliseo, Olivia—left behind,
Brooklyn. The winter trees remember the river sound.
Underemployed all autumn in Ballincollig, I watched the tree tops,
variegated blowing horizons, from the one bench
that hadn't yet been burnt down on night incursions, "reconstituted
from recycled plastic" (sign says), and asked, *Am I back in Ireland*
—Cork, where I am not from? (Evidently.) Lost, the park days now,
these *Away from Desk* severely pruned seven-minute piss breaks
—head set, toggle on / toggle off, digital time card, head set—
to come now into blackbird territory: bill absolute yellow,
and black body dripping, black absolutely, low to the ground
under dripping trees.

I listened for the river, which is continuous,
and prone to flood, and listened to tree sounds, which are partially
ongoing, rising and falling, what is ongoing
intermittently heard behind and within the trees' argument,
the buttress dam hidden from view. It is in Dripsey, lon dubh.

Land

Lagnajita Mukhopadhyay

after Agha Shahid Ali

That sidewalk stretch always ends abruptly in this land—
like rule or an imitation-spreading westward-cleansing land.

Why are the magnolia blooms dripping from the trees;
how romantic the Cracker Barrel looking out at the land?

If home is speckled and I swore that I would not refuse
to go because I had no one to go with to greater lands.

Cars and passing eighteen wheelers and ugly flags, our
wind, rounded beacon rising from golden and hollow land.

Certainly, this country has more guns than people, and
our libraries torn down wrong, big hands, for more land.

Why would you understand? You are this country now,
its servant, its faithful pickaxe as chained down to land-

owner, close that window and turn that down, you claim
to build, I am about to give you some religion, you land-

lord. I read somewhere that America has more museums
than McDonalds and Starbucks combined, story as land-

mine, place as explosive. Hitchhiking in these times is
impossible, they say. When was anything free in this land?

I want to go a place where nothing reminds me of you.
I search the corners and the empty lots, such wasteland,

for unknown. Like the masters. Like the shovels.
The big city street and the dirt road all bleeding land.

I keep swiping my MetroCard at the gas station, he says,
waiting for a change or the right time to leave this land.

I say go now, I say do not look back, not in the rearview,
Lagnajita, not in the dictionary, but in the cold hard land.

Florence, November 3, 1966

Lisa Mullenneaux

A little river that can't be satisfied[1] except
that night when, strophed in each others' arms,
we slept while it rose and raged.

"Worse than the war," we heard next morning,
or during the Black Death—a city of ghosts—
marooned in a sea of mud that dirtied

Dante's skirts as he scowled down
at the birthplace that had abandoned him.
Then the work began: *coraggio, pazienza.*

Shopkeepers tried to salvage inventory,
raking out sludge, while others tended
to the art invalids in basements and on

the walls of churches, bathed in the muck
of sewage, decomposing animals,
black heating oil from busted furnaces.

They called us "angels of the mud."
We only mopped and carried. No one knew
how to save the wounded, the dying.

Mulberry paper, space heaters, glue.
Cimabue's Christ twice crucified is today
a man whose skin was eaten by water,

not by flames (priests catching bits
of floating paint in sieves), a man stretched out
on his poplar cross who says: *attende me.*

1 Dante Alighieri, *La Divina Commedia,* Purgatorio, Canto XIV. *"Per mezza Toscana si spazia / Un fiumicel che nasce in Falterona / E cento miglia di corso nol sazia."*

A Walk That Revealed The Essence of a Woodland

Patrick McCusker

Some years ago, I worked as a naturalist in Ontario, Canada. One of the tasks I was asked to provide was to undertake a survey of plants and animals in a particular woodland. The purpose of this survey was that Ontario Parks needed a clearer understanding of the potential of the entire area for development into a provincial park.

I collected together mist-nets, small-animal traps; butterfly nets, collecting jars and reference books. And a map to locate the place.

It was an old forest with several small streams cutting through it. On one side, it gave way to an extensive area of wetland that drained into a large river in the distance. A scattering of ancient trees had toppled down and were now mouldering back into soil. Nevertheless, they had kept their shapes and had formed long ridges of decay where they had fallen. Upon a number of these mounds a new generation of trees had taken root on what once may have been the bodies of their parents. Some of these youngsters stood over thirty feet tall.

On my arrival I discovered a make-do wooden hut. No need to unfurl the tent. This hut would be my shelter. It was nothing fancy, but it had a sound roof, which, in its entirety, was covered in a thick layer of cushion moss. The hut was no more than a small square room that boasted a tiny window, webbed and re-webbed, from the industry of generations of spiders. A jumble of planks of wood, a table, and two chairs fought for space. And, for some reason, a large unopened tin of paint, rusted through on one side, stood on one of the chairs. This hut would be my home for the length of the survey. A layer of mud and fallen branches, that had accumulated over years, had the door stuck at open. It took me the best part of an hour to clear away enough of the mud to get the thing to finally shut.

The survey work was immensely enjoyable. So, too, was the solitude it offered. Within days I had organized myself into a ritual of rising with the dawn to attend to my traps to see what the night before had to offer. A telescopic butterfly net and field binoculars were constant companions during the day.

A forest is not just a collection of trees. It contains an undergrowth that is influenced by the conditions dictated by the canopy above. And the trees are the guardians and protectors of all within their shade. Together, these trees, and the shrub layer below them, generate a presence and an atmosphere that pervades all.

I knew something of the trees that were to be found in this forest, so I was comfortable in their identification. But the shrubs and ground flora were another matter. The reference books would be invaluable in identifying many of these. For the rarer ones I would need the help of experts back in the office: people with remarkable botanical knowledge.

On the second night I had a visitor. A repeated banging on the door had me out of my sleeping-bag; flashlight in hand. I peered out into the darkness – and down. A large porcupine presented himself at the door and waited to be let in. Clearly, by his insistence, it was his hut before mine. Well, maybe it was, but I had seen dogs, their faces covered in porcupine quills from having been struck by the tails of these animals. So, I had to firmly tell my visitor that he could not come in. With numerous prods from a plank of wood he was persuaded to go away. The going-away, however, wasn't very far. He took up residence in a hole under the hut: no doubt waiting for the pest who had taken over his home to go on his way.

But there was one other adjustment that I was forced to make. An adjustment that was in greater need than dealing with an insistent porcupine – snakes. There is a misconception that all naturalists, and rangers, are fearless rugged types who would think nothing of calling the bluff of a charging bear by standing their ground. Maybe that is true for some. But, never having been put to the test, I am not sure what my reaction might be if that difficulty presented itself. On the quiet I had been advised that a tall tree would be a sensible second option. But, for me, snakes were the big-bear-rush. Whether they were poisonous or not made little difference. Coming to Canada from Ireland, where there are no snakes, had a lot to do with this attitude.

The problem I found with snakes is that they are suddenly there. They make no sound to warn of their coming. If they would only make some kind of a clatter, I might hold a different attitude. But, unfathomable black eyes, suddenly staring at me at close range, was, to say the least, unsettling. To this day I am uncomfortable with snakes about the place. They seemed to carry a cold wisdom from the time of dinosaurs.

But, in fairness to the snakes in this particular forest, I had to recognize that this was their home. The purpose of the survey was to map out the distribution of species so that their habitats would be protected in any subsequent developments into a provincial park. All of that is fine, but I hadn't expected snakes to be living right inside the hut.

On the first day, when I was cleaning clutter out of the place, I discovered three black rat snakes in residence. Each was about four feet long. One was on a shelf, high up. I discovered this when I foolishly tried to remove a flat board above my head. The snake had been coiled up on the board. When I tilted his shelf, he slid downwards and went right over my head. With an experience like that, the work of tidying up went a lot slower. Every board and every plank of wood was treated with keen suspicion.

That black rat snakes are non-poisonous was not much of comfort. I had been bitten by one before, and it hadn't been pleasant. So, like the porcupine, the three of them had to go. Holding my fear under tight control, I grabbed them, in turn, by their tails, and running to the door, flung them away and off into the long grass before they had time to react. That was fine, except that all three of them had a shared attitude towards ownership. This point of view was strengthened that night by a violent thunderstorm, and torrential rain. The rain drops drenched down onto the forest with unbelievable ferocity, and depth-charged every puddle and pond to frighten the tadpoles below. In its fury, it roared against the moss roof and streamed down the tiny window, seeking for places of entry. And all three snakes appeared back in the hut by crawling through several holes in the walls. They were back home, and there would be no more of this throwing-out business, especially with such a storm hammering down outside.

The dread I had was that I would find them in my sleeping-bag for the little heat and comfort I might generate. Searching for a remedy to solve the problem, I noted the large table. The sleeping-bag went onto the table with me inside it.

On the first night, an unsettling thought came to me and nestled, with great insistence, in my head – did snakes climb table legs? I didn't know. Anyway, any bits of sleep I had hoped to gain, collapsed away when the sleeping-bag fell off the table. Where were the snakes? Where was the flashlight? Clearly, it was essential that we have a truce, each party keeping their distance. And, in truth, the three of them kept to their side of the bargain and never bothered me from then on. They were content to occupy the planks of wood at the back of the hut. Each slept in a different area, the locations of which were never far from my mind. I was the lodger in their hut and I had to respect that.

Days passed into weeks. The notebooks grew thick with observations. Using a relascope I took numerous heights of trees, and an increment borer gave me their age. The ease by which some species mixed, or stood aloof, was noted. Hemlocks and white cedars seemed to delight in each other's company. Sugar maple and red maple had more need of light. Yellow birches preferred to stand alone, or to form themselves into exclusive clumps. Red oaks grew in drifts and bands throughout the forest. Speckled alder insisted that their feet be in water, and fought for space in the wet places among giant bur-reeds and blue flag iris.

One of the delights that I looked forward to each morning was the identification of bird species. Birds have personalities: I am convinced of that. Grackles, by the racket they engage in, saw to it that they would not be over-looked in any diary entries. They are mischievous birds brimming indeed with personality – and devilment. Black-capped chickadees are different. They know to be quiet and to keep their distance. But, for all that, they were numerous, friendly and inquisitive. For the entire time I was there, one group of chickadees stayed in a clump of white pine next to the hut. Among other birds: bitterns; bobolinks; ovenbirds; red-winged blackbirds and downy woodpeckers were all recorded.

Herons have always been a favourite of mine. Other than an occasional 'crake', they keep their silence. But, by their size, they would not be easily missed as they carefully pulse past on slow wing-beats, as if they had not entirely mastered the skills of flight. But to see them, dropping down to land with one foot carefully testing the ground before the full commitment, is pure beauty.

Deer were present, but other than tracks, I never caught sight of them. Lynx, too, ghost walkers in the evening, left not a trace of their movements except for small tufts of hair on thorns. Racoons were the jazz band of the forest. They saw to it that they made a great din outside the hut every night; exploring for what they might find through the bits of equipment I had left outside.

Ever conscious of my sharing the hut with the three rightful owners, I made it my particular purpose to carefully map out the strong-holds of snakes throughout the forest so that any developments in the proposed park would not harm their holdings.

Wild strawberries grew in profusion. Foam flowers; Joe Pye Weeds; beebalm and black chokeberry were there. In open spaces, meadow grasses, sedges and Black-eyed Susans competed for space and for the nourishment that the deep loamy soil had to offer.

But, in spite of the growing inventory of things, there was something that I was missing; something that I could not pull into focus. Whatever it was, it seemed to conceal itself behind a fog that I could not penetrate. In my several weeks of living in solitude, this important absence continued to elude me. Yet, it was there, stretching over the entire forest. Through all my observations, and through the growing mound of pressed plants, there was something about that forest that I had not captured.

It brought to mind the discipline of Japanese painters, centuries before, who would go into wild places to paint. But they would not pick up their brushes until several weeks had passed. This would allow them time to absorb an understanding of what they were to capture with their palette knives and brushes and paint. It was only then that they would set up their easels: the time being right.

On the last morning of my stay, when I emerged from my make-do hut, the forest immediately seemed different. It was as though it had decided that now was the time to show itself to me as it really was. This revelation came slowly: nothing rushed. It built upon itself until it was suddenly there in all its clarity. On that last morning, the forest presented itself to me in its indescribable completeness, no part separated from any other. No tree or chipmunk or frog less important, or more important, than anything else. All in their place, none out of place. All were an integral part of the one.

From out of this astonishing insight, the work I had been engaged in over those past weeks seemed trite and meaningless. It came as a shock to realise that what I had been doing was fragmenting the indivisible forest into separate pieces as though that would give me an understanding of its nature. I had been completely wrong. What I had been doing was confronting a great poem – and hadn't realised that. In its entirety, the forest, that morning, displayed for me its true nature: a nature beyond any measurements that I might attempt to make. For the first time, what I was seeing was indeed a poem, and I had been butchering it into pieces in trying to gain an understanding of what it was. A great painting, when viewed close-up, is a meaningless jumble of brush strokes. But when we draw back from it by some distance, we can at last see the unified statement that makes up the whole. It was that profound reality that the forest was displaying for me on my last day there.

I took a long walk, on a now familiar track through it all. I carried neither notebook nor binoculars. On this extraordinary morning it would have seemed improper and tasteless to do so. Never did pine pollen, that rimmed every puddle that morning, seem to shine with such unusual brightness. It was as though each pollen grain was revealing something about the forest that was beyond the need of any inventory in any notebook.

The realisation of what I was seeing, really seeing, left me with an overwhelming feeling of bewilderment. In merely accumulating lists of names, I had entirely missed the essence of the forest in all its completeness. And what was it that I had been missing?

It was the gallimaufry of a multitude of things intensely woven together to make the totality of it all. It was the bark of a fox; the call of a goose over frosted ground; the snoring of owls; the haunting cries of loons, like the wavering calls of the long-dead, that they might still be remembered. All of these sounds were part of that. So too, was the warm breath of deer drifting in the cold air among the trees; the constant choir of frog-song at evening time; the sway of Blue Joint grass; the flit of Meadow Jumping Mice; and the murmuring together of forest flies in flight, in numbers beyond comprehension. Something else as well. The silent breathing of leaves in summer time. Then, the spiralling-down of prodigious clouds of them, their job done: so many leaves, in preparation for winter, to make mulch that others might grow. The spin of whirligigs and the ballet-dancing of water striders on every pond was also part of it all. And, just as important, if more diaphanous, was the caress of the morning mist against the trunks of trees. Drifting too, across the open meadows, this mist, like the soft kiss of snowflakes over each dying petal, gave it an assurance of a job well done. Whispering past the grey-white whiskers of mice, and dragging over the thin sheen of ice starting to form on small streams, this quiet mist gave an affirmation that everything was as it should be. And, above all else, an enigmatic and unseen presence, that understands all and that holds all of it together in its completeness.

In one fleeting moment all of this came together for me on that morning. And it was a feeling that all of this is what we should know if we are ever to properly understand wild places.

When I packed my things that day and got ready to return home, the last thing I did was to replace the mud around the hut door to leave it open for the porcupine.

In writing my report back in the office, I felt like a traitor. I was not setting down the sense of that forest at all. How could I? It was beyond the ability of words to capture what it was that I had experienced in that beautiful place. My report, among others, would be used to evaluate the potential of that unforgettable forest.

Those Japanese painters were right. To understand a place, you must first spend time there. Modern technologies drive our minds to be functional, and only to be functional. They remove all sense of reverence and strip away time: time that is needed to give space for our abilities to wonder. This quickening pace, that no one questions, takes from us the silence, the solitude and the slowing-down of time that is essential to fully understand what can be found in wild places.

I carried out surveys in other forests, but I never again experienced the closeness to nature that I encountered, on my last day, in that ancient woodland those years ago.

STRING THEORY

Pat Jourdan

There are times when my atheism breaks down, like those strange burps when the fridge stops working. You depend on something in the background to continue, unacknowledged, until it does not function. And suddenly, atheism did not work. I wanted to say the rosary, no, more than that, I wanted a rosary.

I wanted my Mummy.

From past visits to the local church, definitely no rosaries were for sale – it was not a shop after all. No shop in town, a mostly Protestant area right down from Cromwell or Witchfinder General days, would be selling a set of rosary beads, not even the punkish off-beat shop where crosses of all sorts were available in all weird shapes and metals.

Searching in the file cabinets at the back of the mind, like all of us, a general pool of unconnected knowledge, I knew you could make a workable rosary by getting some string and making knots to mark the place of beads. I rooted round the shed and found a ball of string. Take a handful, then start – ten knots a bit apart, one knot, ten more, until there were five sets of tens and their interlinking singles. All decimal system, really. Knot both ends together. Then, add an extension, with a one, a three and a one. It was like a living Morse Code. Knot this short length onto the big circle. There was a discarded crucifix somewhere in the sideboard drawer alongside other detritus and that was added at the end of the extension and there was a handmade rosary, the sort a prisoner would make if they had access to string. I was lucky.

Now I could set to praying in earnest again and reclaim some lost part of my psyche. Obviously it was tenth rate, like a rope bannister that trendy architects imposed on families, thinking a wood one was old-fashioned; I was old-fashioned and perfectly happy.

A knock on the door. Lily stood at the step and glided in.

"Make me a cup of tea," she abruptly ordered, without any real greeting.

"OK. It's that time anyway, the boys are at cubs and scouts and I was just going to make some." Lily sat down. Tall, very tall and skinny, as though she had been ironed. Pale as well. More like an ironing board really. We chatted a bit while I produced mugs, milk and teapot.

"I want something to eat," she said, briskly as though I was a servant. Tea was usually the prelude to a heart-to-heart with any friend – but to sit down and start demanding food was different. I produced some toast, a bit puzzled and sat down. Quintessentially English middle class, Lily was usually polite. But tonight she was different.

"Don't you realise? I'm possessed of the Devil?" she said conversationally, finishing off the toast. Her face changed to a sneer. I said, equally conversationally, as though this was all completely normal everyday chit-chat.

"Isn't that lovely! What a coincidence! I've just finished making a rosary. See?" waving the brand-new string. She took it, grabbing it right out of my hand.

"This won't be enough. You'll have to get a priest. I need a priest right now. The Devil is in me." She grew quite panicky and desperate, so even though it was a drizzly autumn night, I got my mac and ran up to the presbytery next to the church up the road. Thank goodness priests have to live on the premises next door, not miles away in the suburbs. The presbytery was down a dark path next to the Abbey. A Victorian Gothic porch sheltered a fake mediaeval door with a long iron rod to pull a bell inside. It jangled loudly.

A priest opened the door, and I entered a large hall, paved with real marble black and white tiles set diagonally. Rich Margo and her husband had the lino version and we all thought that was ultra-trendy. This was real. I garbled that I had a young lady in my house who was possessed of the Devil and she was asking for a priest.

"Nothing to do with us. It's probably drugs, these days. We don't do personal exorcisms just on the hop like this, you know." He went off and came back with two more priests, all of course in black. The three black-suited men against the black and white tiles were like a scene from a 1960s prizewinning Italian film. I felt like a film producer. All three of them argued that she was probably mad.

"But it's not a doctor's she's asking for – it's you she's really calling for. Please, I can't do any more and I've got to get back. My boys are at cubs and scouts, there's no one else in the house." One of the priests hummed and ha'ad, then led me to his car and we drove the short way back. He was not pleased.

When we got back, the boys had returned and the house was full of smoke. Jim and Tony opened the front door, gasping for air, their eyes watering. Luckily there was no hall, our front door opened right into the room, so our smoke drifted out to the dark street.

"She wouldn't let us open a window or a door, she said the Devil would get in." Devils indoor or out, they must be everywhere. Apparently, she had produced several letters from her handbag and had burnt them in the kitchen's big Belfast sink. The priest stood looking round at our poverty. Lily was sitting on the shabby couch in the front room, dress off, just in a petticoat. My prized Anglepoise lamp was balanced on her lap, the light focused on her throat.

"So the Devil can't get in any further." She smelt of something medicinal.

"She went up to the bathroom and was gargling something" Jim said, still red-eyed and coughing. Tony, years younger, was entranced by all the excitement. I raced upstairs; an empty bottle of Listerine lay on the bathroom floor along with her crumpled dress and cardigan.

"Have you used all the Listerine?" I asked. She nodded.

"I was trying to get rid of the Devil, so I drank it all." The priest asked her if she was feeling all right now. So far, he had not said anything holy, nor started any prayers. I rang 999 and asked for an ambulance for someone who had just drunk an entire bottle of Listerine. They were on their way. The operator agreed it was serious enough. Soon two healthy, stalwart, normal men, backbone of the country, were also standing in the front room. They brought normality with them, ordinariness and safety. Lily said she did not have to go with them, she knew the rules.

The priest, now there were six of us plus Lily, felt surplus to requirements.

"I can't do anything here, it's now a medical matter," and he left, while Lily remained tightly holding the string rosary and the lamp. One of the ambulance men whispered to me,

"We need to get her out of here as soon as possible. She's not taking any notice of us, can't you persuade her? Every minute counts." But Lily heard this and said again, clearly,

"I don't have to go with you. I know my rights." I realised that she must have been in this sort of situation before, to know whatever rights she had in the here-and-now.

Sudden anger is powerful. I went across, and reaching down to the skirting board, pulled the plug out and snatched the lamp off her knees. She crumpled then; the lamp had given her both ammunition and drama. Now she was just a girl in a petticoat, looking silly. She deflated.

"All right. I'll go with them. But I want to wear your mac." I'd got her own dress and jacket from upstairs into a plastic bag and now put my mac round her shoulders. The men said I'd best not get into the ambulance with them.

"Better we take over here. You've done enough." Plus, I had the two boys to look after and console in the smoke-filled house. Lily gave me an angry look as she climbed into the ambulance. Next morning on the way to work for the cleaning agency, I went to the nearby hospital, enquiring how she was. "She came in last night."

"Heart attack or stroke, was it?" the receptionist asked kindly.

"Oh, no, possessed by the Devil, they brought her in by ambulance." The woman looked up, startled.

"Oh, then she'd be in Ridgefield, you'll have to get the 27 bus and then change to the 51 near to the trading estate." I'd try it after work. Being a good neighbour can be costly, but I needed my mac back. It was getting to November and the weather was not going to improve. The mental home was set far back from the road. I asked at the desk to see Lily and she soon arrived (with an attendant) in the waiting room. Very superior, as though I had done something wrong. I began to wonder who was mad, me rushing round, frazzled after cleaning three houses, or Lily, tall, calm, and perfectly dressed and cared for. I looked harum-scarum in contrast. I asked for my mackintosh back and she sent the attendant to her room or wherever, and I had to thank them both for that. Lily was apparently angry at me for getting her into all this trouble. It was all my fault.

The string rosary was lost in all the trouble, having done its work and was never mentioned again. I felt for it, so new and with so much suffering it had borne already. The bathroom floor had to be cleaned too and all the house still smelt of smoke, while the sink, even after several scourings with Vim had brown scorch marks where she had burned the letters. The neighbours wanted to know what scandal or trouble had happened. You can't hide an ambulance. It was as if our house was marked. The boys blamed me for having crazy friends. I still needed a rosary and had annoyed the priests.

A knock at the door. It was Lily's mother, a well-dressed middleclass woman, with such a gigantic bunch of flowers that it blocked the entire doorframe.

"You did it! We wanted her to get treatment but she always refused." At least someone was happy. I looked at the flowers, working out which friends to offload some to. They took over the table. We would be unable to eat. Lily's mother was a doctor, so it must have been an embarrassing and challenging situation. No wonder Lily had left home and was living in two rooms round the corner in one of the big Victorian houses.

A day later, another knock at the door. Lily's father. He was a small man, dark, wizened skin. He had a Scottish accent. I knew he was a doctor too and he looked spry and healthy enough.

"I wanted to see you to thank you. You were mentioned in Lily's case notes, they gave me your name and address specially, as another medic." It was evening, the boys were out again. He did not want tea or anything, he said. But he wanted to talk something over with me, something very important.

"You are just the type of person who is aware of other things, unearthly things. You would be well advised to be guided by me, into further fields." What was that? He went on. "I could help you regain your buried gifts, your insight into life itself. I could lead you into the craft of Wicca – true living knowledge." I looked at him. He was mad, even if he looked smartly dressed. But he continued, oblivious. "Once you have the real gift, the entry into the knowledge of Wicca, you will have ultimate power. I can guide you." He chuckled. "I can give it to you. I can tell you, for instance, a group of us, four men, well, we were after punishing someone, so we danced round an empty wine bottle on the table, we sang and then we broke the neck of the bottle and called out his name."

"And?" The thought of four old men dancing round an empty wine bottle was hilarious but also gruesome.

"He got cancer of the throat diagnosed the very next week. Died soon after." He smiled, gleeful at his triumph. I stood up. The atmosphere was tense, deadly; threatening even.

"It's time for you to go. I don't want anything to do with whatever you are suggesting. You should be ashamed, being a doctor and all." I walked to the front door and called him to leave the house. He stole past me.

"You'll regret this. This was your chance, and you refused. You don't know what you've thrown away here."

Boys back, supper, baths, bed – the joy of common routine, our home back on an even keel.

That night, I woke in the small hours to find Lily's father, a sunburnt sprite, standing right beside the bed. An atmosphere of consuming black hunger, like a foul magnet exuded from him.

"Go! Go away!" I shouted, shivering, and then the vision dissipated, fading quickly. I said a couple of Hail Marys to reach safety again, earth and heaven twinned.

I knew now where Lily's Devil possession had come from. She had mentioned her father would be visiting town and that he had gone round and had tea with her that afternoon before her attack. Goodness knows what he had done to upset her so deeply, perhaps wanting to involve her in his crazy network too. How sad, with her own name symbolising whiteness and innocence and her resilience broken down at last.

I wrote to a friend in Ireland, enclosing a note, to pay for a rosary to arrive by post as soon as possible, a real one.

The Unquiet Oracle

Massimiliano Nastri

'Astéras eîsathrêis 'Astēr émós 'eîthe ghenaímēn / Oúranès ōs polloîs òmmasin eís sé blépō.
You gaze on the stars: might I be, O star of mine, / the skies with myriad eyes to gaze on you.
— Plato (attributed), *Anthologia Palatina*, VII, 669

The expected laurel, tamarisks, jasmine. Other plants are unlabeled.
Most are drying out. The south: heat, and carelessness.
In the cave of the ever-present tuff nightmarish scepticism,
The unarguable implications of common sense:
What comes to light is dying; the final pang will heal from tragedy;
The world won't stop; react or not, it gives meaning.
Could one tolerate more answers, reality bared of details?

Stating *vita mutatur non tollitur*, that time has been unchained, that is
A lordship of delusion - is it, then, a real mystery
That one sees you, seeks your profile in every person?
In one playing hide and seek with a baby girl, behind a straw hat.
This unknown infinite in a chosen possibility is not an echo,
Or a reflection of spiralling dragonflies over a gargling fountain.
One can lose what was never had, but an unshared farewell remains harsh.

The cooling wind from the cave proves these wants are as worthy as
The cicadas' crackling, leaves too dry to read. Agreed, but
Obduracy keeps names, memories alive, not at peace, at one
With this dripping emptiness. Another call may return to exist.
In this ageing universe, the night sky is to the stars what gaze is to desire.
My offer is humble: a twig of gorse for the honeybees to linger on,
Fragrance better than incense, and citron's seeds. Their rest might take root.

French Press

Dan O'Brien

I didn't know how so they showed me. This was the Huguenot Quarter and they were students at the nearby art school; they were working here for money, I presumed, to pay for paints, brushes, canvases. They pitied me. I'd speak only to order. Then scribble my love letters. Reading eclectically in modern Irish poetry. Acclimatizing, convalescing; and all the while the fragrant first cup … second and third pouring gritty and charged with more tight-fingered mind-lightning. Because I was half-expecting (hoping?) I might someday find a family, I noticed a young mother breastfeeding in an aureole of sunlight through glass, shading her areola and her baby with an unfolded *Examiner*. I was at least vestigially Catholic, seduced by the votives the art students glided along the tables at the end of the day. They let me stay. I remember them now because I am newly in remission and coffee can be my only vice. (Some doctors say harmful, others helpful.) Only one time do I recall becoming visible to them: climbing the steps to the balcony seating when I tripped and wiped out with my tray—glass shattered grounds scattered spreading brown on stone … They cleaned up before I could and brought me a new one without asking.

Glenveagh

Nathanael O'Reilly

Ingest rowan berry jam
from the glen of the birch.

Nourish yourself amidst heather.
Inhale the tears of god. Caress

moss growing on towering
Scots pines. Tap birch for syrup.

Inspire the apple-skin
scent of woodland sorrel.

Cradle in the arms of ancient
oaks watching red deer graze

beneath rowan's nests. Lick
mist dripping from ferns.

Connect with ash and holly
like climbing ivy. Absorb

healing nature like sphagnum
moss holding water. Evict

the sins of past histories.
Heal yourself in Lough Beagh.

Another Beginning

Triin Paja

I ran into the forest to hear the cuckoo.
the earth was boar-bruised,

the roots marred,
raw. boar,

I also prefer to terrify
than be ankle-shackled by longing.

then the cuckoo called out.

there is a field inside the bird,
and the idea of time.

like the bird, I want to inherit nothing
from mirrors.

I want to run into the forest,
again, again—

there is honor in waiting,
but also a certain death:

wake up, beloved.

I ran into the forest. I sent,
foolishly, a kiss to the cuckoo.

I adored my foolishness.

I smelled a twig of jasmine
and my face fell into it:

yes, death is in me, but it is not my name.
I unfurl in all directions—

this has no end. becoming is a river.

U.S. v. [HIM]

Andrew Payton

The author inscribes a quip about beauty
in a book about cages.
A childhood friend spent his twenties
in a cage
reading Russian existentialists and pleading his case:
I did not do
what they say I did. I wrote letters,
sent books,
a few times visited through glass.
I imagined him
like Han Solo in carbonite with an itch.
Years later
nearing release
I read the transcription of his trial:
he said he was most attracted
to kids ages 9, 11, maybe 8.
By this time I was father
to child.
Him: *the intention*
was fictitious. Judge: *We are not*
like pigs
hunting for truffles buried in briefs.
Where in the body
does one summon absolution?
Later, he is free.
He passes me on my bicycle,
a woman asleep in the passenger's seat.
I love you, dude, he calls.
I burrow into the back of my skull.
In a book about cages
the author inscribes a quip about beauty.
The beauty
of the world, he writes,
of our world. He writes my name
but is he speaking to me?
My ribs too are my animal's cage.

A countrywoman's child in Dublin

Cathy Power

There is scant solace in the wild
for a child born between the canals.
No matter how my mother curled
her lip and sighed recounting tales

of country childhood, I was and am Dublin.
Warm evening brick around an open window
over Mountjoy Square was always up there
with picking blackberries on her quarry lane.

The creak and gush of canal locks where dirty
pike and mullet skulk are match for any midland
river brimming with gleaming trout and salmon.
It's on old concrete at the Bull Wall,

with scutchy grass and rat-infested rocks
my head clears, my tears fly in the wind.
Thumping across the wooden bridge
my eye won't seek the North and Binn

Eadar's yellow gorse but drifts South
where oil tanks and chimneys make my city
heart slow down. My horizon's made more lovely
when daylight fades and orange glows from piers

and jetties mirrored in the channel in between
No gull-nested crag, but yellow concrete bunker
invites me to dip in Dublin Bay, with women
just as cynical as I and *just as old.*

How to Unbury a Whale

Matthew Carey Salyer

As promise & premise of this lyric I'll
try to be or not to be

helpful, wise or unwise, however you'd like.
Whatever will frighten the horses free.

This is the third hard year of your inhibition.
The first you'll outlive as mutineer,

howling in the moving castle of your name.
With or without animus, anima.

Here's the line where I say my body's becoming
fast my fäTHər's (I fear), the rubrics

of being or not being oneself, of being unencumbered,
seeming altogether less urgent in praxis.

If true, if love collapses
even the vastest distances between us, it must be

that somewhere your Hy-Brasil, your utmost,
exists within this poem's spellcast.

If I shut my eyes to you,
the inner world of their lids ambers with hearth.

Almost the brink counties. Imagine
milk thistle slinks from the monochrome shore

burning after a raid. Blood sheds
whatever was fortified of its cold its birdly attire.

Ash on the earth's wool skirt.
Across a distance beveling into the elective past,

the northmen try to unbury a whale – in the pasture
I groom your name like a foal that is or is not on fire.

Ballistic Sonnet

Samuel Samba

The guide says '*Imagine a crime scene*', & I shave my fist into a
knuckle—bulleting past a row of bodies,
the way each clenched finger troubles the atmosphere before hitting
the loamy-soft field:
a metonym that tells ballistic apart from a short-range missile.
& when my fist flattens its trigger-soft fold, I clinch the expertise of a firearm
while holding onto this place, this one-time home of gossip & foul
language
in the name of a SWAT unit—emptied of prisoners since the last firing squad test,
making leftovers of the sergeants who go neck-deep, sorting piles of
abortion pills & loaded contraband stowed in wagons
that leaks freshly into a tidy mess of Indian hemp shoved behind an armored
tank.
the guide proposes a second description: think of it as a shotgun approach to the
boy's quarter where exhibits lay in similar pattern of grief.
blood-stained shirt tying the moment. fingerprint samples
stashed on each other. each mannequin, standing animal-close to a
ruptured limb. gunpowder smeared on a longline of rifles. what is a crime scene
without one, anyways? twelve of them placed in standalone order of
what bullet makes it into the next loin. on forensic ground,
a life-size dummy wrecked beyond repair. two ruptured feet & a severed
arm, dead with rot. I question its leftover stink. the grief lies in the asking. so, I've
learnt to
empty my doubt in words, to hunger for answers. a missile trails
me down the bulletproofed stairs, injuring holes into the wall plate that eats fire
daily without a scratch. shellings, plastered to the soil like sewage piss.
the recoil
drags me by my youth, to places bronze sharpens into warfare, till the flint shines
dagger-bright—it turns into accidental discharge. taming a weapon
all year
renders you stone-cold & motionless. the guide fills up his cartridge,
empty prayers into
a Kalashnikov & in one deathblow pulls the trigger. the rough impact, accentuated by
a primer spark afflicting his lung: a hiccup, blent in some tonic sol-fa
ranked in the hierarchy of G major. his lieutenant lips—a seizured vibrato. their acoustic
positioning, aimless as a scattergun. name it a ballistic retort & life

goes on, or off. when the canon ball meets my fist, & its two-tongued clip folds in cowry
shape, I mutter '*boom*' amidst incantation. although, days after, I
purchased a cowry sized chain laced with cannon balls: all bullet-fit, bone-clean &
tortured into finesse.
yet, beauty won't erase the horror I faced at SWAT unit. perhaps, a live band once
occupied this building, or why else does peacekeeping demand a
tonic sol-fa & acoustic positioning to tell us: *we're all answering to a certain*
breathlessness, with guns shouldered as a refrain. twice, the guide
said the team attempted to rescue a girl bloodletting under a tout. upturned the rogue,
to meet her plowing her body with a rod.

White Trash Prods
Heather Laird

I grew up on an Irish farm, the youngest of eight in a church-going Protestant family. The farm was in the northwest of the Republic and, like most people in the vicinity, my family rarely ventured across the Border, though two of my sisters would later get jobs in Northern Ireland and settle there. There were few Protestants in our home town, so we travelled every day to a Church of Ireland primary school in a nearby one. It was a two-teacher school when I was there, with numbers dipping on occasion to levels that just about warranted the second teacher. Shortly after I left, it became and remained a one-teacher institution. My father supplemented the farm income by providing school transport, picking up local Protestant children in a baby blue Volkswagen minibus. He had bought it second hand for a good price, and the other children and I would compete to see who could close its stiff sliding side door with the fewest bangs. The milking had to be completed before the school run and milk delivered in white plastic cans to some of the neighbours so our contingent rarely made it to school on time, often missed the first hour or so.

The Protestants in that nearby town were better-off for the most part than the ones around us. I drove through the town quite recently and was surprised by how dilapidated it seemed, but it was fairly prosperous back then, known for the good grazing land that surrounded it, its weekly market and substantial department stores. Country people travelled there from miles around to shop, especially in advance of weddings and other special occasions, sometimes treating themselves to a cup of tea in its (by Irish standards of the time) posh hotel. Some of the town's biggest stores were owned by Protestant families. I went to school with the offspring of those families. I also went to school with children from a family that those better-off Protestants and their offspring looked down on. Two of the boys were in my year; the oldest had been held back. "Mr Can't" and "Mr Won't," the teacher in the Big Room called them. "You're Mr Won't," she would say to the younger of those brothers, "because you have a brain in your head but you just won't use it." "And you're Mr Can't," she regularly said to the one who had repeated the year, "because, you do try, god love you, but you're too stupid to ever learn anything."

Some years ago, I came across the American author, Elizabeth Strout. To my knowledge, I've never met a so-called "white trash" American, but Strout's recurrent characters from that background seem familiar to me, and I feel anger, shame and culpability when Strout touches on their treatment at school by teachers and fellow students. The brothers in my primary school class are foremost amongst the faces and names from my childhood and adolescence that come back to me when I read Strout's novels, and encounter in their pages Lucy Barton, her siblings and her cousins. As fans of Strout's writings will know, the Barton family are economically impoverished and widely rejected in the community. Lucy discovers as an adult that her brother threw up every morning for one whole year before school. Given that the Barton children are routinely bullied there for dressing "weird" and smelling "funny", his dread is hardly surprising. "No one [is] too poor to buy a bar of soap," Lucy's sister is told by a teacher in front of the class. "We were trash," Lucy says in one of the literary works centred on her, "that's exactly what we were." This declaration is in retaliation to her mother's description of Elvis as "a big old piece of trash" who appealed to "cheap people." Her mother retaliates back, reminding Lucy that their ancestors were early Massachusetts settlers. As reinforced in all of Strout's "Lucy" novels, Lucy's attempts to leave her childhood behind will always be hindered by the extent to which she remains traumatised by it, and by a lack of commonality, with regard to life experiences and cultural references, between her and most other "successful" Americans. When Lucy's niece, a minor character in the Strout oeuvre, is called "a piece of filth" by a teacher in a moment of anger, we see that the Bartons continue to be shunned, notwithstanding Lucy's use of the past tense when proclaiming her family's "trash" status. Moreover, while this young woman is clearly talented, her life, the reader is led to surmise, will follow a more common trajectory than Lucy's in that her potential will remain largely unfulfilled.

When I recall those brothers from my primary school and their two younger siblings, I can picture them clearer than any of the other children at that school, but I'm not sure how accurate my memory of them is. I suspect that it is shaped as much by how they were perceived by others than how they actually were. It is my recollection that the youngest of the four always had a cold and snail trails of snot on his sleeves. I doubt he was the only child in the school to use the arm of a jumper to wipe a particularly drippy nose, but his is the only snotty sleeve I have a clear image of. When my own daughter started primary school many years ago, I stuffed all of her pockets with tissues in the vain hope that she might make use of them. She had a tendency at the time to employ a handy sleeve, either her own or someone else's, to clean her nose. Even though I knew, logically speaking, that she wouldn't be the only four-year-old starting school that year with poor nasal hygiene, in my gut I still associated stray snot with the ostracisation of small children, and it terrified me to think that she might be targeted for it, like that little boy was. I remember all four members of the family wearing glasses. The frames were identical; there was, I think, only one type available to children for free then. Sometimes the glasses got mixed up and one of them would be beaten for not being able to see what was on the board. But it was really just a pretext. In their case, the mildest of offence warranted physical punishment. I don't know how often they were hit by the teacher. Looking back, the punishments seemed relentless, with the four siblings spending much of the school day either dodging blows or cowering beneath them. One of them, possibly the youngest, had a habit of nervously grinning whilst being beaten, which tended to aggravate the teacher and prolong the attacks.

But I also remember seeing and hearing the boys in my class from that family transform when talking to my father. He would light up a cigarette, lean against the van and chat to them while waiting for the children from our town to load up. He might ask them about an older male relative or the harvesting of the turf that year, and they would answer him back the same way that I had heard adult men speak to my father at the creamery or out on the land. Before my eyes, they grew in stature, and any advantage, academic or otherwise, that the rest of us had over them in the school building itself was, in those moments, outweighed by how much older they suddenly seemed to the rest of us. And I sensed then that while my father wanted his own offspring to have a very different life to those boys, he also despised us just a little because we were children in a way that they were not and he had probably never been. My father was a life-long avid reader, particularly of large tomes of military history, but his formal education finished at fourteen and from then on he had worked on the land. In addition to his duties on the family farm, he had intermittently sold his labour on the farms of others until the ownership and full income of the family farm was passed over to him when he was in his late twenties with children of his own.

One day my father came into the school to complain about pupils deliberately jumping in front of the van whilst he was trying to park it. When the teacher pointed to the brothers in my year, asking whether they were the culprits, my father responded that as far as he was concerned they were the only mannerly children at the school. The rest were savages, he said, nodding very pointedly in the direction of a group of boys from the more well-to-do families in the town. It was that lot over there, he went on, who had no respect for anyone and were always messing around the van. That day some of the boys from the wealthier families were beaten for the first and only time by the teacher, while the two brothers looked on in amazement. It is perhaps not surprising that one of those brothers showed up at our house in the middle of the night years later, asking my father for help of some sort. He had already had a run-in or two with the police by then, though I'm not sure that had anything to do with the help he was looking for on the night in question. My father is dead nearly twenty years so I can't ask him about what took place between them, but I suspect that he sent the young man away. We weren't well-off, but we were "respectable," and my father wouldn't have wanted to be dragged into anything that risked threatening that "respectability."

When reflecting on this ostracised family, it has often seemed to me that to be the kind of rural Protestant in Ireland that can be looked down on is similar to being the kind of rural white in North America that can be looked down on. In both cases, something else is at play, a larger dynamic that this treatment is secondary to. In North America, that larger dynamic has to do with the country's history of slavery and an associated long-standing assumption of white superiority. White people whose way of life and socio-economic standing challenge that supposed superiority become objects of scorn, in the past sometimes even referred to as "white niggers" to indicate the extent to which they undermined the socially-constructed white/black divide that underpins racism. The closest – though by no means identical – historical correlation to this in Ireland is the colonisation of the country, with religion functioning as a marker of difference between coloniser and colonised, and Irish Catholics often figured by British political and cultural commentators as racially suspect. Though religious tensions in Ireland, south of the Border at least, have been less extreme in recent history than racial tensions in North America, I suspect that my teacher's irrepressible urge to beat and humiliate those brothers and their younger siblings stemmed at least in part from a deeply-ingrained belief that, as Protestants, they were letting the side down.

The Protestant secondary school that I attended as a boarder in the 1980s was in a larger town than either my home one or the place where my primary school was, further northwest but still in the Republic. The pupils were a strange mix. There were some posh prods, as we called them, but back then at least it wasn't the school of choice for affluent Protestants. There seemed to be an unusually high number of students who had been expelled from at least one other school, or maybe they were just the ones that I ended up hanging out with. A substantial number of the day pupils came from Catholic backgrounds. Some of those had liberal parents who would ideally have liked their children to have a non-religious education and considered a Protestant school as near to that as they could get in the locality. Others had parents with social pretensions who considered a Protestant school more prestigious than a Catholic one. I remember finding that amusing at the time, given how many of us were mere bargain-basement prods, nothing like the ones from the Big House. A parent who clearly fell into the latter category singled me out once at her teenage daughter's birthday party to ask where my mother clothes-shopped. Sensing that this was a very different activity to my mother's occasional replacement of individual items of wear in the one clothing shop in my home town that catered for women, I blanked, not sure how to respond. I suspect that this was just one of a number of occasions when the woman in question wondered whether the school was, in fact, the right environment for her offspring. There was no religious divide as such in the student body, but there was a division between some Protestants and the rest of us, Protestant and Catholic. Don't get me wrong! Individuals were ostracised or bullied for all kinds of reasons, but this was different. I doubt any of those Protestants came from backgrounds as economically deprived as that of the aforementioned children I went to primary school with – indeed some of them came from families with considerably more money than mine – but there were similarities in how we thought about them and how we treated them.

And I use the word "we" deliberately. I don't think I was a ringleader. At least I hope I wasn't. But I don't remember ever trying to intervene. I wanted to be popular and I was always in the outer circle of the "cool" kids. I was also friends with people I liked who were not considered "cool," but I would never have risked my position in that outer circle by aligning myself, publicly at least, with anyone who was especially targeted. While in no way constituting a defence, I suspect that the isolation I had experienced in the years before I went to that school shaped my behaviour whilst there. Though my family was a large one, I had at times lived the life of an only child in that the biggest gap in age was between me and the next sibling up, and as I approached adolescence I was mostly on my own in the house with my aging parents. Since I didn't go to primary school locally, I had no friends nearby. My mum and dad were hard-working country folk, who would no more have thought of organising a playdate than they would have considered travelling to the moon and back. In the end, I grew so lonely that I cried until they agreed to take me out of primary school a year early and send me to boarding school on a partial scholarship. Once there, I rarely studied. Instead, I put all of my energies into making friends, and had considerable success in that regard. I was more than aware, however, that this institution, while a haven of sociability for me, was a living hell for some, and ultimately I must have been willing to accept a system that worked to my benefit, even though I could see quite clearly its potential to destroy others.

There was a group of female Protestant day pupils in my year whom we collectively called "the smellies" – I cringe as I write this. I'm not sure how that particular "slag" came about. I suspect that one of them had a mild case of B.O. for a brief period in first year, which is not unusual amongst hormonal young woman, and that was that. For the most part, these pupils came from farms and villages on route between the place I went to primary school and the larger town where my secondary school was. I'm not sure how they got to the school. Perhaps they came together in a van like the one my father drove. One of this group left education early to get married. Some of us got it into our heads – I don't know how – that it was an arranged wedding and that the soon-to-be husband was related to her, maybe even a cousin. We dressed up our negative response to her marriage in a veneer of feminist concern, but ultimately it tied into some notion that we had of those pupils being weird, in a hillbilly kind of way, and most likely inbred. Given how interrelated Irish people from a southern Protestant background tend to be, it seems ironic that we would have chosen this particular form of insult! A further irony is that the term "hillbilly" – widely employed in North America to refer to poor whites from the Southern highland regions – has possible Protestant Irish origins that we were unaware of when applying hillbilly stereotypes to some of our fellow secondary school students. One theory regarding the word and concept suggests that it originated from early Protestant settlers from Scotland and Ulster who were referred to in this way to reflect both the areas in the US where they ended up and their historic associations with William of Orange.

The aforementioned day pupils who were the butt of such stereotypes at least had each other and went home at the end of the day. Boarders targeted in similar ways had it considerably tougher given how little reprieve there was. One pupil was called a witch for most of her six years at that school. She came from a relatively remote farm on that aforementioned route; my memory is that her family lived in a mountainy area, but while the region is certainly hilly, this recollection might have had more to do with how we perceived her. She was small for her age with masses of hair. Her first name sounded as if it came from another era; indeed, it may well be back in vogue, given the current trend amongst young parents for giving their offspring "classic"denominations. Her hair style and clothes were also very old-fashioned, more like what we would have associated at the time with an elderly female relative than a contemporary. Most of us had short hair and wore drainpipe jeans, bleached or ripped. She wore frocks and, for more casual occasions, cardigans and flared slacks. Flares have been in and out of fashion since the late 1970s, but for much of the 1980s they were an absolute no-no in Ireland. She maintained that old-fashioned look throughout all or most of her schooling. Her cultural references singled her out too. At a time when musical preferences could make or break you, she didn't know which bands were "in," and didn't seem to care. The slagging never fully let up, but I think a grudging respect for her unwillingness to conform kicked in towards the end. Most impressively, she managed to turn the witch thing to her advantage in those final school years. If anyone was particularly unkind to her, she would take on an otherworldly persona, delivering a very plausible and personalised curse that few were willing to risk.

I met her on a train a few years later. She told me that she was studying to be a teacher in Dublin. She was reading Noel Browne's *Against the Tide,* as so many Irish people were at that time. I had read it the year before when it first came out and so we chatted about the book for a while. I shared with her the story that my mother had told me when she had seen me with *Against the Tide,* of my grandmother losing a sister to tuberculosis and then, for fear of my mother and her siblings getting it, keeping the windows of the house wide open throughout their childhoods, even on the frostiest winter night. And I remember at one point early in the conversation reflecting that we didn't seem to have damaged her too badly and feeling relieved by that, my guilt somewhat alleviated. But a little later it struck me that she was a more conventional, flattened-out version of herself. In all the years that we had hounded her, she had never changed fundamentally. But here she was: looking, acting and sounding more or less like any other young woman on that train. And I wondered whether she had reinvented herself between school and further education, as some people do whose adolescence was particularly painful, or whether she had had an even worse time in her first year or so of college than with us, and was finally succumbing to pressure. Either way, it felt good to be sitting with her and I was glad that she seemed happy to talk to me too. I was conscious that I probably wouldn't have been as forgiving if I had been her.

I think it was a year or so later that she killed herself. A second cousin of hers, who for similar reasons had also had a difficult time at that school, came to the Rathmines flat I was living in at the time with a boyfriend to let me know. Our paths had crossed in Dublin some time previously and, having discovered a shared love of books, we stayed in touch for a while; I still have the copy of James Joyce's *Dubliners* that she gave me for my 21st birthday. She said – if my memory serves me right – that the young woman had been home from teacher training college and had asked her younger brother to show her how to use the shotgun. I remembered him vaguely from school: a quiet boy, also small, who, as tended to be the case, was automatically targeted from day one because of how his older sibling was perceived. Later that weekend, she had gone with the shotgun to one of the outhouses on the farm and blown her head off. And I thought how awful it must have been for the brother and that it didn't seem like her to involve him in her death in this way, but then I reminded myself that I didn't really know her; that I had never bothered to get to know her; and that I still found it hard to separate out who she was from how she had been viewed by others.

Lucy Barton reflects in one of Strout's novels on the countless ways that we find "to feel superior to another person, another group of people." "It happens everywhere, and all the time," she surmises, and is the "lowest part of who we are, this need to find someone else to put down." While there is certainly truth to this, such universalist statements mask the extent to which the extreme and unrelenting ostracisation of individuals and groups invariably has a structural or systemic component. In the case of the fictitious Bartons, their persecution is linked to their membership of a grouping – white settlers – that, as Lucy's mother recognises, had an historic advantage in a society founded on slavery, but occupying the lowest rung of that privileged set. The brothers in my primary school class and the teenagers that I encountered later on who were treated in similarly disparaging ways are not part of any conventional story of southern Irish Protestants; a grouping that as a whole benefited from the colonisation of Ireland. Big house narratives, often suffused with a nostalgic glow, tend to dominate that story, with the less well-off Protestants featured in the Big House novel invariably belonging to formerly ascendancy families and now living lives of shabby gentility. Except perhaps for the bouts of isolation that I experienced as a child, very little in such narratives speaks to my experience of being raised as an Irish Protestant, with regard to either the commonality of Irish experience or the specifics of what it is like to belong to the lower rungs of an historically-privileged sector of society that still has notions about itself. And so it was in Elizabeth Strout's empathetic yet complex fictional explorations of the intersection between social class and white privilege in North America that I first found echoes of the individuals and life experiences that made the most impact on my childhood and adolescence.

A Boneyard of Flesh// Post-War Trauma

Nnadi Samuel

my joy is a dead language
—Khalypso

I.

yet, a nameless gravestone rolled between cold war & now.
a maddened apparition, manifesting from the boys' quarter of my pain, of each
bullet-eaten cave by the roadside—razed down to a crumpled papier-mâché.

my brother, ulcering out of my grip the way a blood-soaked font detaches
from the page of medical record as a pulsing illness, or a budding lump.

'*tonight stinks like an open sore.*' & in the wild gift of event, a scar
shapeshifts towards healing. violence scrawled in its wake.
& styling its way into turbulence—it thunders through a ribcage.

2.

there: the hurt, bruised to whitening. there: the chewed carnivorous
water—yawning a boneyard of flesh. the shore is language dead enough
to drown in, to squeeze to a thorough blot & punctuate with rumpled bodies
of my race. their negritude, whitewashed into effervescence.
our crude & grief-infested dialect like yellow bile, unsettling the tongue.

3.

post-war, a fragment of our surname drowns in bulletproof soil. brother,
deboning the wild knit of concrete. he yanks off a body from its loamy
existence, & the air reeks of Ma. a boy ago, he grieved the dry season
of his infancy into a bonfire with no bones to hawk the flame.
amusement parks grew less amusing—slaughter driven by the urgency
for blood. carousel, racing same way into the stomach of an ambulance.

4.

the kill are smuggled in body bags on trolley, headed for nowhere.
grief grows surplus & doubles over with loss. a lad, foisted to a
stretcher—brandishes his dislodged wrist as a teenage gadget,
& grieved a purple sore boomeranging everywhere across town.

what bullet colors my accent? the impact, too sporadic to chew a whole
lineage. what language meets a bomb halfway between *beauty* & *boom*?

5.

lights-out: a soft shadow loiters the lone street, scavenging the bloodshot
yard for tampon. & in a sleight of hand, unshelves a pregnancy test-kit.
a sergeant pounds her from behind—as if I mean, without a gun.

[prenatal]: she binge slowly on the fat bile of loss. gloom, trellising her insteps.
[postnatal]: she craved fish stew on empty cartridge, bullet-shaped torso of
a lamb—marred in gunpowder. see how sorrow makes a carnivore of us.

beware of me. grief burdens my core. a fetus once there has gone missing
& not one blood to show for it.

6.

say: the ancestors have no hand in our woe. say: their spirit misjudges the bullet.
resurrect their ancient loin, for each fallen shape to plead in cold-blooded language.
say, I was the voice peeling the wind, there's the probability you'd find me un-alived
by a missile or near miss, or vowel explosion. my tongue: a dead language.
phoneme, plastered to my cheek. its cruel alphabet—liquifying my gum,
as sadness foams in maritime rage.
the saltless blessing, roaming in my mouth like rotten carcass.

7.

in the year of disaster, your ghost come home to roost on the eve of May:
an earthshattering sound—headed towards chaos. at the crack of dawn,
you're boar leaping toward light: a violence dead on arrival.
in a country that speaks fire, '*my joy is a dead language*'.
a dark accent, scrubbing grief on pink tongue.
the colonist's verb keep revamping more corners for us to die in.

I wear my mouth in reverse, & gun a pronoun down in one shot. cheers to
how we self-identify with hurt: a bullet for dodged bullet—in this ghastly language.

say, you find harm to outpace. thank the fitness of foot,
thank the femur & the calcium that fills it with tonight's horse race.

8.

there, my dead relatives unfurling like a peeled chorus.
their unrehearsed glow—putting light to guesswork.
dear brother, happiness is a far cry from here, & at the rough edge lies
a matchet moon—the way the sky slit supplication into sore throat.

you shape out, voiceless from the onslaught.
see, what troubles your larynx: medieval's wreckage.
a cannon ball, gunning for your lung.

for Erika

Jaric Sarmiento

we meet for the first time, her neck is sunburnt, then she was there, with me, nine years old, underneath the pulsing sun, hidden, behind dry leaves and torn aluminum, runaway, she held her hand out, muskrats, scraps fell to empty triangles, "your hands are the same size as mine," the night freezes, we're talking for the first time, arranging a playlist, to score tofu scramble, cooking to indie pop, the room expands, like galaxies, her freckles ripple, like a rise, from fish, feeding, and she was in Japan, with me, under the bridge, holding me as I twiddled with the wounds on my thumb, defecting from class, tears, the water pulsed against the pillars, cigarettes, flying, with the wind, the rain battered, abused, the pavement, bruised, her cheeks pressed against mine, I heard the four chords, there's a fishing hook hanging on a tree, by the river, the sun peeks from the flora, armadillos and muskrats, the smell of cicadas, the swallow, cheek raises, we kiss, a ballerina, twirls on the river, the forest alight, with aurora, she stood opposed me atop a cliff, I had just gotten my license, there was a lunar halo, I didn't leave a letter, ink drips, the air bit the skin, I looked at her and she glared back, eyes like concrete, the pavement, hurt but unwavered, arms wide, feet firm, "no one's ever looked at me like that before," she's having a panic attack in our airbnb, chest pulsing, breaths scraping, her throat, trying, to calm down, she's listing five things she sees, the ceiling fan, fuzzy blankets, paintings of burlesque shows, the dust rising like twirling ribbons, us at the center, five things she hears, the praying vents, storms, convening with rooftops, remnants of jazz, the silent lullabies, I say I love you, she feels, my lips on her shoulder, our cuddling hair, my heart, at the rate of 96 beats per minute, her fingers strumming my stretch marks, the air feels soft, I was locked in my closet, the bruises sank, the blood, tasted like iron, I saw her, sat beside me, rocking me back and forth, crying with me, I heard her, "it makes me really sad that you went through most of your life thinking that you couldn't be loved," but I don't, she was there, and she had always been there, I felt her, her hands, the same size as mine.

Castor & the Huntress

Mara Adamitz Scrupe

When a Frenchman trades with them, he takes into his services one of their Daughters ... who is familiar with the Country, undertakes, on her part, to serve the Frenchman in every way, to dress his pelts, to sell his Merchandise for a specified length of time; the bargain is faithfully carried out on both sides.
—Sieur de Dièreville, *Relation du voyage du Port Royal de l'Acadie, ou de la Nouvelle France,* published at Rouen, 1708

furthermore that yellowish exudate – not to be confused
          with castor oil – that the animal uses to scent mark
its province – flows from sacs located next to two anal
          pouches found in paired cavities at the root

of its tail   & the pretty gap-toothed girl with the gun
          – bird hunting in the 40s – she damn sure knows
who she is & what she wants   but she has no idea where
          she'll go   or who she'll

be eventually there will be tales of her exploits
          turned into such & such an allegory even a myth
or two but not a single parable – though she'll attend mass
          as she was taught to do/ she always   will –

but you mustn't anticipate a moral to this story/ meanwhile
          the feverish hunt for pelts drives the New World trade
& drunk & naked coureurs de bois will marry – *à la façon*
du pays – lovely maidens in exotically exuberantly beaded
          moccasins – what better way to cement the bonds

of commerce – though one will object/ running away/ only
to be caught & killed as notice or admonition & another once
          -girl not so pretty anymore – but still not too hard
          to look at – ruffles walking the exultant flowerheads
of an Estonian flax field – forb waves rollercoaster

around her – rising & declining/ undulating like cerulean
          sex   & this woman who is not a girl anymore

considers an option/ a choice/ a might-have-been recalling
          her mother the Huntress/ Artemis of rowdy woods

– she wears her big brother's baggy wool jacket/ his flap-ear
plaid trapper hat – & how she loved Chanel No. 5 & the rough
way-up-north Minnesota of her childhood – some ninety years

back – & whistling swans & the other/ the trumpeters
          especially – the latter believed now to be extinct – both
disappeared from their historic breeding grounds/ killed
          for food their territories long ago plowed

under & she thinks she remembers reading that the earliest
          Europeans coming to that frost-bound glacier-dredged
dominion – French fur traders   acclaimed casualties

of *l'ensauvagement* – sought beavers most supremely
          for castoreum – from that creature's Greek name
kástoras – collected from its sex glands for its leathery carnal
base note/ prized ingredient   of the parfumeur's art

Burial Rites

Lorna Shaughnessy

I. The Reluctant Iconoclasts

We left the toughest decision till last:
having neither faith nor space to house them,
what would we do with the holy statues?

The PP advised: bury them, but break them first.
I take the easy task of digging the hole, my sister
grits her teeth and takes hold of the hammer.

I dig deeper than needed. Not even the smallest
shard of our mother's faith will be exposed
to scorn, whether unintended or in spite.

Reverse archaeology. After years of peering
at remains of pots and figurines rescued
from the earth with scalpel and trowel,

glued and labelled for display in glass cases,
today, our hands lay to rest in a fresh grave
the plaster fragments of what we have broken.

The Child of Prague's blue painted eyes
look up at me, still serene, but I am grateful
Mary's head is bowed; I cannot meet her gaze.

II. The Right Thing

The day before we buried our mother's statues
we visited our sister's week-old grave
where wreaths withered on the parched clay.

It was a botched job. Earth piled unevenly
on one side, a gaping, unfilled hole at her feet.
We sighed, concluding our tip had fallen short.

The wrongness of it all sat heavy on our chests.
Once we had given the saints a decent burial
in the back garden, we returned to Milltown

armed with spade, hats and sunscreen
to do right by our sister, breaking up
the baked clay, taking turns to shovel

and smooth till it resembled a dressed bed,
something that could be called a place of rest.
Two sisters straining in time, jaws clenched.

Colostrum

Cassie Smith-Christmas

During this breast-feeding webinar
my mind slips to saints and their miracles

of lactation: Brigid for example whose cows
could be coaxed to milk thrice a day;

or Ita, who suckled a giant beetle at her side
bulging with blood, her skin its flotsam.

And when the other nuns killed this monstrosity,
she mourned and begged God for the Christ Child,

to hell with kings and men of earthly power:
she had Ísucán, her fosterling, nestled at her breast.

And long before his sojourn on the fire-flung sea,
at Sliabh Luachra her *dalta* Brendan drew milk from a deer.

The midwife online is describing that first moment:
the bitter scrape of air on skin, the shock

as the baby emerges from its luscious ocean
into a world unknown, a world of edges.

Yet how those nascent drops let them know:
it will be okay.

And for the first time since my belly has swelled,
I let myself say out loud: we will be okay.

In Cahoots with the Night

Alyssandra Tobin

I walked my dog and talked sweet on the phone. I left a man's house and bought myself a leather harness that buckles around my neck, circles each breast. Sometimes I think I'm no good – tears pricking eyes, nails scraping palms kinda worrisome. As in – why can't I stomach loneliness. As in – what stopped that man from killing me. As in – who let me own a dog in the first place. I can't be trusted. Quiet voices of the mice who live downstairs, stop telling me about the hole in my chest and how dirt can't fill it. I've heard it all by now. Slick wisdom and celestial reasonings. A handful of fortunes torn from stale cookies. The knock at the door when no one's expected. My ma calls me too trusting, too naive. Jaq calls me out on my addictive personality. I lie in bed with stuffed animals and dog hair. I gesture towards wholeness and shy away at the pivotal minute. Paul calls me from jail and I don't pick up I don't fucking pick up. Call me kind one more time. Somebody. I'm running out of excuses again. I'm turning fallow. Running out of tap water. Sick to the gut with vibrations and murmurations and all sorts of unspoken history. It's a growing season thing, I can tell you that. My bones are stretching out the skin. My mind is caught on the hook of summers at the garden. My heart – oh yeah, my heart is sneaking away, a lone dog dodging the blow.

Silver Lake

Heather Treseler

Newton, Massachusetts

I.

That summer, we felt we had discovered the lake—
we lay claim to it as if we could, as if it were not
a public park but our own personal oasis where

we might continue our decade-long argument
about irony versus tenderness, and whether
cleverness or gentle feeling might redeem us

in the end. Must they always be opposites?
I asked, puffing as we nudged our bikes up
and over the hill. Or are they paired house

keys—without which we are homeless
in a world of sharp insistent edges, work's
endless demands? The grind of bike gears

and city horns were my answer as we spun
down to the bathhouse and fell into the spell
of wordless custom, threading locks through

frames and ambling to the end of the warm
wooden dock where we dangled our tired legs
into the spring-fed lake, six tall men deep.

We watched the last hour of light glimmer
across water, a frail ladder reaching toward
the opposite shore with its scab of beach,

stand of trees, and a young boy busy with
his shovel: *bent to it,* to his self-appointed
task, digging a portal to Sydney or Santiago

with all the pleasure of purpose, his face
and torso curled over a patch of earth,
little priest in his liturgy of make-believe.

II.

The boy wasn't ours. Not the curve of
his delicate shoulder, lathed in late day's
lambent light. Not his small legs, sturdy

in their industry. Not his faraway look,
his *idée fixe* to save the ancient castle
from its moldy moat of alligators,

to be crowned prince—or discoverer of lost
elixir, alchemical gold. To rescue a story
forgotten or untold. Not ours, this boy

with his sweet shag of bangs and laughter
at what he conjured from wet sand, shallow
water. That winter, we had learned there

would be no child and a door shut
with finality. The future carried
no blend of our faces, high arches,

knock knees, dark eyes, your or my
unruly burr of hair. Yet now we saw
children everywhere. They lacquered

us like waves of glass, mirrors of lack.
But to live is not to garner all you desire,
to roil in your narrow shell, hard limits

of the actual. Might this sorrow improve
us? Chasten our complacence, startle
settled assumptions? Around or beyond

this absence, might we reach nearer to
each other, shorn of ready-made future?
We ached, without irony or answer.

III.

We came to the lake wanting reprieve.
Vestigial, this yearning for water's release,
as a certain kind of luck or leisure was receding

from our reach. The local field guide noted
the land was called *Nonantum* or "Bless it"
among Algonquin who knew its sylvan birds,

sloping hills, each freshet stream. It was theirs.
Then, in 1654, Thomas Wiswall bought it from
Governor Haynes. *Bought* the books say, but it

was theft: nothing given to those from whom it
was taken but dispossession, disease, and death.
Boughten they said then, calling it Wiswall's Pond

as if he had dug it with shovel and bucket to quench
the thirst of milk cows, draft horses, two wives, ten
rosy children. On these banks he built a meetinghouse

to worship an imported god. Ritual conviction
a form of method acting in the colonial theater
of brute belief. We read the history, felt in it

our own zeal for taking, our endless want. How it
scants tenderness, the forgiveness of skin pressed
to skin as lovers knock at the door of the other,

begging to be released from the self, let out—or is
it let in? Up close, you had begun to evade my gaze,
staring into a vague middle distance at something,

or someone, a watery mirage unnamed. Does love
fulfill an eternal law, as Kierkegaard claimed, or does
the chronic gnaw of its hunger leave us maimed?

IV.

Every couple must have their pocket of third things,
mutual loves beyond pets, sports, or hobbies—a child
or god in whose name a shared faith becomes a kind

of blessing, a pattern to the aches and ways of days,
a reason and need beyond the self, beyond the fickle
calendar of desire with its seasonal duck blinds,

its pratfalls and subtle turns. There must be a third
truth or beauty, worthy of mutual liege and liturgy,
its ceremony lent to the otherwise rude run of time.

Without, between us, the hallowed-out place for gods
or the constant measure and hungers of a child, it
seemed parts of us lie shipwrecked at middle-age,

a beach littered with something unspent or unwaged.
No one reaches forty—or fifty—without some dream's
phantom limb, some parallel reality of other choices,

spouses, the practice of other ardors. We took our
bets, and we revisit the waters of this neighborhood
lake, swimming in draughts of its black ink, grateful

and yet yearning for things we cannot pull within
the orbit of our reach. We travel from dock to beach
and back again, taking in the sacrament of light

ablaze across darkening water, two bodies upheld
by buoyancy of learned skill and habitual appetite.
We swim briskly the lake's cold middle, against

the risk of sudden cramp or distress. Watery death
sly beneath our feet, we feel, anew, our vitality,
our fragility, the luck of our ease and ordinary love.

V.

We had abandoned our work with the zeal of kids
for recess and spotted, among the trees, the blue
ruffle of the lake, its sequined summer dress.

Settled on the dock, our feet bared to the mouths
of pickerel, we watched the sun set in haze, its
hyperbole of fire pinned by the Baptists' spire.

Once, they brought brethren here in all seasons
for immersion. Come winter, they axed a portal
through the ice. A sinner waded to ankles, knees,

then waist, stammering a creed in benumbing chill
while a minister lowered, then raised, the doused
gasping head. To be rinsed, for once, of all fear

and troubled doubt. In that era, they called it
Baptists' Pond (and Baptists' Bathtub) but
in the next, they renamed it Crystal Lake,

farming the pond for hunks of ice, extracted by
horse and tackle, turning frozen water into dollars
in the old American way—whereas, we'd like

to think, we are patrons of its beauty. Our irony
admixed with tenderness when we come to its
silver eye to watch it blink. Done, for a little

while, with labor that earns our keep. We bathe
in its mirrored clouds but do not pray or, like
supposed witches, sink. Yet we are a pagan pair:

a bucket and shovel on a rough-hewn beach, bent
to a purpose we hardly know, but that our salt
craves a depth of water with the hunger of belief.

Slow Learner
Mary Morrissy

It was a phone-in radio programme and a woman was explaining about the problem of expressing victimhood. If you don't have the words you can't formulate the experience, she was saying. She was an academic doing some kind of research so she had all the jargon. Though the word that stopped Freddie in her tracks wasn't jargon, it was a plain word in plain sight.

Bullying.

It was a light-bulb moment, another phrase Freddie had never understood until then. She stood poised by the kitchen table – she was clearing up after lunch and she had an empty coffee cup and a crumbed plate in her hand. The moment became fixed in her mind, like other significant memories, like when she had lost her virginity. (Bed-sit, Dublin, after a party, late 70s, not Brendan; she can still see the floral knickers she'd worn which she immediately threw in the bin.) She sat down as if she'd heard bad news and felt a sinking sense of doomy knowledge but it wasn't in her head, it was in her stomach.

Is that what it was, she thought to herself with a kind of detached wonderment. Is that what happened to me?

The hardest part to swallow was that it wasn't just one isolated incident. It was her whole life.

She listened to the rest of the programme in a daze. It was, at least, comforting to know she wasn't the only one it had happened to. Loads of women phoned in to relate their bullying experiences, but they'd known what it was while it was happening. Unlike her. But, at least, it meant that it hadn't happened to her because of who she was. Winnifred Daly, a fat swot, useless at sports and no dramatic talent. (When she had auditioned for a small part in the school play, an orphan in a musical, her depiction of terror had reduced everyone to helpless mirth. She who actually knew terror.) But her biggest shame was that it had taken her over 40 years to recognize that she'd been bullied.

It turned her into a slow learner.

She did nothing with the realisation, partly because it made her feel so stupid. As if she'd found soft porn in those outer reaches of the TV channels with the high numbers and watched the heaving flesh waiting for the sex scene to be over.

She didn't tell anyone – well, who would she tell? Brendan? He should understand, particularly now. Explains a lot, he might say, and nod his head to imply thoughtful empathy. He's totally insufferable now that he's training as a shrink. At 55, after a life in IT, he decided to switch careers. Or diversify as he calls it. She loves him, of course she does, but the thought of her big-boned, lumbering, affable husband listening to people's problems with his fingers steepled makes her want to snort with laughter. As if he was running a help desk, only this time to fix humans. Up to this, Brendan has had only a nodding acquaintance with his subconscious, but then who was she to talk?

Was this the kind of thing Brendan's clients were telling him, she wondered. Even if it was, she didn't want to have him explaining her life away on the basis of the actions of two spoilt girls who'd turned her schooldays into a misery. She reasoned with herself that it couldn't have been that bad, if she hadn't realised what it was until she heard a stray remark from a so-called expert on a cheesy talk radio show.

Could it?

Down through the years, she'd heard dozens of people talk about bullying at dinners and parties – boys grown into men glorying in recounting how they were belted by Christian Brothers for being late or missing homework, or merely being alive. Or beaten up by their peers because they wore glasses or spoke with a lisp or were the teacher's favourite. And women arguing that girls were worse because they ganged up in spiteful covens to undermine, mock and exclude the lesser mortals, the girls with braces, the girls who smelled funny. Freddie had never seen herself in any of it. She's even read "Cat's Eye", for God's sake, and even then she hadn't twigged. Because she thought she was simply being picked on.

Bel and Eva picked her, picked her out. They pretended to like her, sidling up to her at break time and inviting her opinion on the Bay City Rollers or the Eurovision. They had a superior game of German Jumps on the go. Freddie was no good at it, although given her clumsiness you'd think getting her feet tied up in intricate knots would come naturally. But it was Bel and Eva asking so you didn't say no. See, she thought she was being smart – she knew they'd pick on her if she didn't comply. But by being asked in, she had lost any allies she might have had, girls who might have been genuine friends. They pulled away because they sensed betrayal. She'd gone over to the dark side, sold her soul to gain entrance to the golden circle.

Once inside, you were deemed to have been granted the great favour of Bel and Eva's company, and then the demands started coming. Little errands – run to the tuck shop and get… Loans of money – I've forgotten my bus fare and then you'd see your sixpence being eaten in the form of an ice cream or a chocolate bar. And still she knew they sniggered behind her back at her frizzy hair and her girth.

Then they moved on to homework. Did you do the comprehension question in English, have you translated your Latin? And because she was now technically a friend, she couldn't refuse. The only subject they couldn't pick on her about was art which was impossible to plagiarise. Was that why she chose it as a career? Because it was the one thing she couldn't be bullied out of it.

Throughout her teenage years she'd lived with that sick feeling that went with being picked on. It was a turnover in her deepest innards and too much spittle in her mouth. Bel and Eva were like a gun-metal sky hanging over her head, but in her stomach they were vitriol. Then one Monday morning when Eva cosied up to her and said simply – have you got your German homework, she suddenly saw red. Why? She doesn't know. And why then? – she doesn't know that either. The rage came directly from her tormented gut, by-passing her brain altogether. She looked Eva straight in the face and told her to fuck off. Something about that obscenity – a word she had never used before – made Eva take a step back, as if she'd smacked her. She remembered Eva's very pale eyes under a glossy fringe widening in shock at the expletive, particularly coming from Freddie, who was seen as a "goody-goody".

Theirs was a school that was intent on breeding young ladies and this was such an outrage that Eva reported her to the head nun for using bad language, even though this risked her and Bel's behaviour being unmasked. But in their value system, Freddie's sin was the more grave.

Mother Berchmans had a smooth, untroubled face which she cocked to one side like a friendly question.

The question was why.

But Freddie didn't shop Bel and Eva – it didn't even occur to her. She had four more years of secondary school to get through.

"I lost my temper," she said.

"But why?" said the face like an ad for Palmolive.

"I'm having my monthlies," she said.

"But where did you hear such language?"

And she couldn't say – you haven't heard my father.

"On the tele," she said.

"One of the foreign stations, I presume?" Mother Berchmans said.

She'd got 500 lines and had to do clean-up after domestic science for a month. But Bel and Eva never came near her again. One curt fuck-off was all it took.

It might have stopped them, but Freddie has experienced that sick feeling many times since and she has never again retaliated, so, in fact, it had changed nothing. It just drove her courage underground.

At 15, she went to extra art classes with Miss Gunn in a dingy little studio at the top of a house on Charlotte Street. She used to get sick before the class and after. Dread and relief, a familiar cycle.

Everything about Freddie seemed to provoke Miss Gunn, her timidity with colour, her size, her determination to keep her head down, not to draw attention to herself.

"Speak up," Miss Gunn would say when Freddie was forced into answering a question. Questions from Miss Gunn were like gauntlets thrown down.

Once, during the break, Miss Gunn halted in mid-conversation with the others who were all much older than Freddie, and turned to her.

"You eat like a cow," she said.

Freddie was battling with a toffee.

"Disgusting," she spat. "Anyway, look at the size of you, you should be staying away from sweets."

There was a ripple of laughter in the group though Miss Gunn was overweight and slovenly and had greasy hair.

Freddie swallowed the gnawed mess in one go.

Miss Gunn's thin spindly mother, who helped out in the studio, saw the episode and tried to make it up to her. She and Freddie were rinsing out the oil-coated brushes in the spartan kitchen set so low under the eaves they had to stoop over the sink.

"You mustn't mind her," her mother said, "she gets frustrated, takes it out on people, feels her work has never been recognized."

Freddie Daly knows what that's like. Now.

At art college she did her thesis on "Ailsa Gunn; a painter eclipsed".

Her final portfolio was a series of miniature crucifixions, but with female figures on her crosses. No nails – she couldn't bear the violence; sometimes she had to look away from too graphic depictions of crucifixion that showed torn and ragged limbs, the rust-red blood. She preferred quieter renditions. Dali's bloodless *Salvator Mundi*, for example, the entire world viewed from Christ's point of view high on the cross looking down. Above it all, not mired in it. For her portfolio she decided she'd do a complete stations of the cross depicting women's torments. The scourging at the pillar was done with the flex of an iron, the crowning with thorns was a beauty pageant tiara, Veronica added to a female Christ's pile of soiled laundry, Simon of Cyrene helped with a double buggy. I'll be the next Judy Chicago, she thought.

When she left college she survived for a bit on small residencies and drew the dole. The long anti-social hours in the studio made her feel justified in her choice of life's work but she never found her artistic theme. Maybe she hadn't given it enough time. On her own, her imagination flourished and for the first time she had no dread, no fear of what others might say, because there were no others.

But she needed money. She started guiding at the National Gallery and found she was good at it. She did kiddies groups and adult enthusiasts and she liked how she was left to her own devices. No one monitored her lecturers (or off-the-cuff commentaries more like) but she got the best feedback. People said she talked about art in a way that was comprehensible, made them "see" more. She was particularly kind to fat children and lone men, of whom Brendan was one.

After the radio programme she looked up Bel Figgis and Eva Mulhone on Facebook. Bel owned a restaurant. She'd been featured in interviews in the Sunday supplements. She ran one of those chi-chi places with one name, "Soup" or "Spoon" or somesuch. But it had gone belly-up in the crash. Eva was a champion for disabled rights. She'd had one of those births that had gone wrong and her eldest boy had been catastrophically affected. There were pictures of her outside the courthouse when her case against the hospital was settled. No sign of a husband. Couldn't hack it, Freddie had heard on the grapevine. But neither of these life experiences could be seen as punishment, could they? That was just shit happening.

When Brendan came in from seeing clients, he parked himself in front of the television. She was in the kitchen making dinner. She said nothing to him. She was still a bit aghast about the radio programme. It was as if a portal had opened up in her head, through which the evidence poured like sugar through a sieve. Everything was of a piece when she used the bullying filter. That time when she was teaching in secondary school and there was a student – Kathryn Dunville – who reported her for bullying. She wasn't likely to forget that name in a hurry. The girl had a hare lip and Freddie knew she shouldn't think it, but it was like her whole personality had been knitted up around her flawed mouth. Everything that came out of it was crooked.

Miss Daly had bullied her, she said, had humiliated her in front of others.

I corrected her, Freddie said, she was wrong.

We don't use the word wrong, the principal said, that's not a word in our vocabulary.

I am the teacher, Freddie wanted to say, isn't it my job to put students on the right path, not to allow them to labour under misapprehensions?

She's targeting me, Kathryn Dunville said, she's never liked me, she's never given me a chance. She called my paintings crap.

Well, that was a downright lie. But Freddie found herself unable to fight back. And she wasn't able to see clearly enough to say – this girl is targeting me, can't you see? It's the wrong way round.

In the end she left the school with the cloud of an official enquiry hanging over her, which is still rumbling on even though it's years ago and Kathryn Dunville is now a 30-year-old woman.

When she went to call Brendan for dinner, he was scrolling on his phone while in the background a documentary about St Peter played out unwatched. She found herself arrested by it, watching silently from the door. She's not religious, mind. Gave that up years ago, painfully, and the separation hurt so much she couldn't afford to get involved again, even if it was only for the comfort of communal worship. Some famous actor with a moustache was tramping around Rome and Jerusalem trying to fill in the blanks about Jesus's most trusted disciple.

St Peter, apparently, didn't quite "get" the whole Messiah thing, and he was forever going off the rails. He chopped off the ear of the servant to the high priest Caiaphas in the Garden of Gethsemane – who did he think he was, Van Gogh? – in a bid to halt Jesus's arrest, nearly throwing God's highly planned scenario out of kilter. Then later he denied he knew Jesus in front of everyone in the high priest's courtyard and only stopped when the cock crowed three times. Just as Jesus had predicted.

Like her, St Peter was a slow learner.

And like Peter, she was apt to betray people.

She remembers, out of nowhere, Johnny Fedrigoni. They'd had a thing at college, an innocent courtship which she couldn't quite trust because she thought him too good-looking for her. Son of Italian parents who ran a chip-shop, he was rangy and warm-skinned and brown-eyed. A mop of curly black hair and a puckish smile. Her heart seizes just remembering him as he was. The graceful heedless beauty of the young. But her lack of trust had broken them up. She just didn't believe him when he declared his love. She couldn't envisage them together because he was part of some golden circle she had already ruled herself out of.

Years passed and they met again. Or rather, they didn't meet because she organised it that way. It was at the funeral of a friend of theirs from college, Jem Lovett, who hadn't made it past 40. The church was packed because Jem was the first of their contemporaries to go and they all wanted reassurance, so the funeral-goers milled around the hearse in the churchyard, loath to let Jem go because they'd have to face up to their own mortality. There was a lot of laughter, enforced gaiety, a *we're all fine* vibe, while Jem's wife shook hands and his children sobbed. She saw Johnny in the distance, enormously fat, a belly on him like a meal sack, a double chin, a dishevelled air, shirt buttons straining, tie askew. Is that my Johnny, she thought, no, it couldn't be. She could see he had seen her, but she pretended not to see him as he made his way laboriously towards her. She ducked behind the crowd and left early rather than face this wreck of a man. She was ashamed of how he looked now as if it justified how poorly she had loved him. She'd rather betray their love than be seen with a fat man.

Still waters run deep, is how Brendan described her. Mars in the 12th house, the astrologer at Pam's hen party said. There's great power in it, she'd said, there's steel, but it's often about suppression.

Suppression of what, she'd asked the woman who had platinum hair and wore a garish smock.

Rage, she said.

The evidence just kept on piling up. The art shop boss who told her she just wasn't up to the job, wasn't ever going to make the grade at selling. His repeated assertions were self-fulfilling. Her returns got worse and worse, until she had to leave. Exerting pressure is what adults call it. Exactly like bullying children. They couldn't be called out on it, it's what they were supposed to do, it's what the whole system encouraged. Dog eat dog. If Freddie had fought back, she'd have been mistaken for shrill or neurotic. Or pathetic.

Her last job was at the New Masters Gallery which saw Brendan through his counselling course. Her boss, Billy Stone, was in his thirties, a man who presented a boyish bonhomie to the world. His self-deprecation was legendary – if he'd been an old-fashioned woman, he'd have batted his eyelashes and made a moué with his lips. What am I like, he'd say to cover missed openings and bad hangings. And then he'd go on to give the impression that he was surrounded by fools, which meant Freddie. He affected a civilised tolerance towards her, as if he'd given a second chance to a friend of his mother's. But behind her back he referred to her as if she was disabled in some way, a basket case, someone whom he'd been lumbered with, although she did all the programming and took on the weekend work when he was swanning off to conferences and making media appearances. She had trained as an artist, she had the qualifications; he was a mere manager. But he treated her like a skivvy and she acted like one. She zipped her mouth and held her tongue.

Blessed are the meek, isn't that what they say? And that's what she is. Meek. But she'll get her reward in heaven, won't she?

In the end, even Brendan said, leave that job. He's always made allowances for her. Her rackety mothering of Pam, the long period being out of sorts as she weathered all the indignities of the female experience, the murderous pre-menstrual tension, the gunshot wound periods and then on into the mood-storms and incontinences of menopause. He put it down to her artistic nature, though she was an artist no longer being one. That had, somehow, fallen by the wayside. That wasn't Brendan's fault; she'd done that all on her own. But standing behind him now in the TV room, the back of his head visible over the chair, that kindliness in him she'd always been grateful for, now with a top coat of waxed professional concern, makes her want to chop his ear off.

"Dinner's ready," she says.

What is she to do with this new knowledge? She's gained nothing from it. The opposite in fact – she's been robbed, her memories all repurposed into a depressing, repeating loop. It reminds her of listening to the Gospels in church when she was a kid, where so many things seemed only to happen to satisfy the prophets of old.

The day after the radio programme, Pam arrives with news from the battlefront of contemporary mothering. Freddie has always been slightly afraid of her daughter because of her forthrightness, her sense of certainty.

"Tilly's been bullied," Pam says matter-of-factly. Tilly is Freddie's 12-year-old granddaughter.

There it is again.

"What?" She tries to keep the alarm out of her voice. Is this history repeating itself? Is meekness genetic? Has it skipped a generation?

"Don't worry, I've dealt with it," Pam says.

I'm sure, Freddie finds herself thinking.

"Her best friend bad-mouthed her to someone else on Tik Tok. Luckily, Tilly told me about it."

"And what did you do?"

"I got on to the mother immediately. I mean, it's alright to have a row with someone, even on social media. But you can't do what she did with a third party. For everyone to see. That's bullying."

It's as if the scales have fallen from Freddie's eyes and now it's everywhere.

"It's simple netiquette," Pam says. "What am I saying? It's common decency, isn't that right? You taught us that."

Freddie looks at her fiercely capable daughter with her brusque, no-nonsense mothering and thinks she didn't learn this from me. Even Tilly knows more about self-protection than her grandmother.

"Alright, Mum?" Pam says looking at her oddly.

I'm proud of you, Freddie wants to say, but doesn't. Because what she means is that she's proud her daughter is nothing like her.

The man who spoke playground

Isi Unikowski

Just there on the rise, before the road descends
into older suburbs on one side, where new estates
have replaced the pine forest where the kids once
threw sticks into a creek now turned into a street name,
my daughter and I have come to a small playground.
Above us a shade sail, like the wing
of a huge raptor tethered to creosote-dark posts,
strains toward the Brindabellas
as if casting the shadow of a cloud on their side.

Why does the mention of *Antrim Road*
seem to evoke so much more than
the name of the road that runs past us here?
Famine and dispersal, certainly, even when viewed
from so far away, the way so much of Canberra lies
compact below us, lending itself to such speculation.
Does that mean such resonance can't be summoned?
Can *Cotter Road* never be given the shape in your mouth
that *Raglan Road* takes in mine?
(After all, Cotter was an Irish settler; and 'Antrim' means 'a ridge.')
Howls from the RSPCA's kennels,
as if Dante's Inferno lies just behind the Maccas over there,
suggest not. Suggest

I come back to now, come back
to the equipment pearled in frost, the swing's
slight movement from the wind's touch, or perhaps
my daughter kicking off in distraction,
the ranges' lilac cummerbund in the distance.
The shade sail above us points to rain drifting in
along the river corridor, over the observatory that squats on its hill,
over the glowing brake lights of miniature concrete trucks
heading to the outskirts, over days
that run like a film coming to spool's end when they're happy,
or turned over one by one like photos in an album when they're not,
over this place graced by a name without resonance,

only by time passing
with the sound of a magpie's wing
cutting the face of a diamond
from the morning's cold quiet.

Two Poems
Patricia Walsh

Love Being Invented

Not necessarily smart, but streetwise, at least
If it were easy, everyone would do it, you know,
Sleeping by numbers, the warmer the better
Signifying nothing, picking apart plagiarism
Gone before it's seen, this rolling tide
A resounding "no" before the show even begins.

Luxury chattels to bribe for better occupation
Being gorgeous on sight, crassly going on down
Sacrilegious confessions doing no favours
The popular lynchpin still calling the shots
Noses kept clean at least till the wedding's over
Schizophrenic dreams rolling out the garden path.

Time and again, the roping-in calls it's trajectory
Not flinching in its design, ambidextrous, perhaps
Vegetating at will, behaving out of sorts.
Eyeball meeting prizes, straight up in severance
The walking death exploding, gathering sympathy
No one comes back, or returns from there.

Dictating what is useless, what's called for is never here,
The promised-for convention never called here
Village idiocy, mistakes shot over dinner
Enough to exact revenge on a misguided kiss
Snakes in the grass still being absolutely free
A bedroom design, a singular rotten hoping.

Voice Over

Grasping the nettle over these tax returns
Speculating over benefit, in live stream now,
Time-travelling deluxe, the rubbished ending,
Formulaic timeserving's rummaging through cross
Heightened lights arrested, catching you there.
Fearing the ridiculous, bruising the fragrance
Dark matter over days, complexion scarred.
Stretching in to the dusk-like days, writing itself
Guided by a voice-over, formulaic announcements,
Walking past deadlines performs the common touch.
The garbled redemption on the sly of working,
Whatever wanted, got, on pain of disintegration
Untitled carnage measuring the rich clique
Not mattering somewhat, muttering to the joke
Limits to form on even a tawdry poise.
Proving it is yours, smothering too much,
Staring at the wrong time, unable to read
Sleeping with the bone structure, starved to fit
High-water beauty never sounded so sweet,
The good news about retail that always clicks.
Washed clean of salvation, studying the irrelevant,
Sanitatized extremities, the time being fled,
Ropes into quiet disaster, exonerated quickly
Coughing up judgement where slightly adjusted
The jibe writ small, turning the air into voice.

Pale and thin as a crescent moon on my bed, you tell me about Titan

Monica Wang

On Twin Earth flows water by another
name; methane forms lakes and rain on Titan

a moon rather than The Moon, you argue
while moping over it like a poet, writing page

after page though you refuse to write me
emails or poetry. I sit in a closed(-lipped) environment

unable to exert enough pressure on you
to choose me over otherworldly bodies. Your expression

when you talk air currents over Titan and Earth
tropospheres and thermospheres and something-spheres

exerts too much force on me instead of passing
overhead with the inverted seasons or washing away

in tumultuous seas. In a thought experiment we might see
three hundred more sunsets-sunrises together. Under the lights

I avoid your blue-green eyes for the last time—they're cold
and only distantly wavering. On any other moon

there exists *an I* who wouldn't miss you.

Exist Strategy

Patrick Wright

After the last photograph she took from her hospital bed

I stab a knife in a kitchen's surface—an existential protest. Or an artist's statement?

I tried to fight & the assailant was invisible.

Now even baby carriages stink of nihilism.

I confide *I want the whole world to burn.*

I'm sick of being a plaything of the gods. They pull my strings just because.

They're capricious & wrong to leave us with such quandaries.

I want to fight with Zeus.

I reckon if I pump my muscles up, I'll go the distance.

I haymaker the door to be heard in Hades.

I beat my pillow with my fist. Here is the heart space.

Awaiting blood tests was like Russian roulette. I won't be scared like that again.

Ours was a war I couldn't win.

Now I know it destroys all I invest—like a toddler attacked by a dog, handcuffed to a fence.

I could do nothing save for making ice pops. I made the best ice pops.

I wanted to jump on a hand grenade, & no hand grenade.

I am the wound & the blade.

No more chemical cures, swimming in ice, helplines…

Friends accuse me of self-sabotage.

I resent the re-wiring taking place—how it's change or die.

Aching Embouchure

Ellen Zhang

On the car ride to clarinet lessons, my mother and I fight over
her insistence in me translating for her at the grocery store.

We speak in her mother tongue, my first language, reason
for my English as Second Language classes until second grade.

My syllables dry like persimmons in the summer heat of
anger as curtness and English unfurls from my tongue.

I hurl hurt at her by dissecting her pronunciation, rearranging
her grammar, and fixating on every flaw in her syntax.

So easily I can make my mother's face slip itself to close.
She must wonder how she grew a part of herself so foreign.

I wouldn't understand her pregnant silence until I stepped foot
onto unfamiliar soil where I stuttered. Words elusively evading me.

Even after my trip to Peru, Spanish strictures around my uvula.
Even now, it cuts my tongue and hardens in my esophagus.

My mouth fillets words like fishbones, small but sharp. What did
I know of shame that threads and traps itself in my mother's mind.

My mother tells me about a new coworker's rudeness
without using the word racist or disrespect—calling it what it is.

This time exercising language not as sword, but as shield.
Rage roots and gathers in my fingertips as I type *Dear Human Resources.*

The truth of the matter is language is a scarce resource. Impossible
to wield it correctly if you forget that my mother is human.

Blood Pantry

Lucy Zhang

The day you bleed means you're ripe for slaughter, Mother tells Daughter. Mother opens the door to the pantry built into the exterior wall, structured with venting to let the chilly, foggy air flow and guarded by mesh to prevent flies from entering, a cooler that looks like a pigeon coop or where you'd stuff duck meat tied with twine, left smoking in a cardboard box. *In you go to relieve the heat,* Mother shoos Daughter in. Daughter hunches her back and watches her head because of the wood slat shelves, her body crammed in the bottom two thirds of the pantry, where the cold air circulates, barricaded from the heat rising to the top. Sometimes you can nip the bleeding in the bud, freeze it out before you plump and soften like white, fuzzy peaches, suffocate your blood vessels like you'd strangle snakes before they can be fileted. Mother closes the cabinet door and waits for winter to pass, and though it's never too cold or too warm in the house, the house is without ventilation—the dry heat gasps through vents. The house is sealed from the outdoors, not a single breath able to seep in and whisper lies to Daughter. But the pantry should be cold, freezing even. Mother doesn't dare open it until winter is over, else Daughter might end up a slab of meat. She is supposed to emerge sharpened, gossamer, exquisite as water runoff grows an icicle.

Antarctica
Jeanne Shoemaker

The front door is steel, bolted on the inside in two places. The social worker scrunches her eyes, as if she's looking at a puppy. She speaks with a singsong delivery. "You have relatives, friends to stay with?"

I have relations. We're a whole tribe, scattered across the country like buckshot. I've stayed with most of them, one time or another. I turn up on their doorstep in the evening, after sleeping all day on a bus, park my suitcase behind me so they don't see it first thing.

Except for the scratching of the social worker's pen, the room is silent and under lit, like a funeral parlor. She hands me a form and I scribble my name at the bottom. Then she scoots her chair closer to mine.

"You can stay for a week," she says loudly, as if I'm hard of hearing. "Then we'll try to get you into something more permanent."

A burgundy shawl covers her thick shoulders. It looks handmade and her hair is long—dirty blond streaked with grey. She's an old hippy who crochets and wears flowing clothing. Everything about her swirls and makes me dizzy. She thinks if I tried harder that my life would be fine.

"Only here a couple of days," I say. Why would I stay? I'm not a housewife married to some fucker who slaps me when he gets liquored up and then storms off in his car.

The social worker blinks then starts in on a rehearsed speech about what I could do and what I should do, but I've heard it before. I wonder where I'll go next—after I get myself cleaned up and my lip heals so people don't turn away from me so quickly. She's chattering away like a mynah bird, making it hard for me to think.

I think about Antarctica and the eared seals. I wonder why there are eared and earless ones. Even in a world of endless possibility this seems farfetched.

My name is Lily Lucas, a name that embarrasses me each time I say it, each time I write it down. My mother named me Lily and my older brother Luther. Luther Lucas is the stupidest name in the world, stupider even than mine. I am thirty-two years old and sitting in the reception room at McDougall House while the social worker checks me in. I spent most of last night in the emergency room waiting to get my lip stitched up.

I started stealing when I was five—crayons from Sunday School and then from kindergarten class. I took the broken ones, figured I was entitled to them because they weren't very good. I smuggled them out in my coat pocket and when I got home filled in my coloring books. But sometimes I just ate them. Aquamarine was my favorite.

The water in Antarctica is aquamarine in the shallower parts, closer to the ice floes, but only in the summer when the sun warms it by five degrees. The temperature varies between twenty-eight and thirty-four degrees Fahrenheit, making it as much as seventy degrees warmer than the surrounding air. For penguins and seals, it's like a hot tub.

I stayed away from my family as much as possible. My parents didn't notice unless I wasn't home for dinner. I was my older brother's punching bag, but he didn't miss me when I wasn't around.

My church-going father, when he was in a bad mood, which was all the time, but especially after he had a few, was easy to dodge, but I couldn't avoid him at the dinner table where he sat, bread in one hand, fork in another. He ate a whole loaf at every meal, using the soft white bread to push and sop up his food while he eyed us, waiting for a mistake. There was always one.

Every night I said two prayers, the Lord's Prayer and the Children's Prayer, but at the end, when you're supposed to bless everyone, your mother, your father, your grandmother, I prayed that when I woke I'd have a new family. I'd still be me, but everything else would be different.

The leopard seal is an earless seal. It is sometimes called the sea leopard and is the most aggressive of all seals and the only one that eats warm-blooded prey. With powerful jaws and long teeth, it even eats other smaller seals. It also eats penguins. Waiting under water near an ice shelf, it grabs the birds as they enter the water.

"Dinner's at six. You help set the table and clean up. Tomorrow, on the bulletin board, you'll find a list of chores. Lily?"

"Great." I need her to stop talking, hand me the pamphlet, and leave me alone.

"Keep this up, next time I see you I won't be able to help. You need friends, a job. You need to stay somewhere."

She stares as if she knows everything about me. Maybe she thinks I got what I deserved, that my fat lip was my own doing, like I walked into a door. And it's true—I did start the fight last night. I do not feel sorry for myself.

Finally, I can go to my room. I call it the honeymoon suite—on your first night you sometimes get a nice private room. I lie on the quilted periwinkle blue bedspread. A head pokes into the room.

"Want to use the laundry? We have clothes here, some that would fit you."

There's blood on my shirt and I didn't have time to pack, so yeah I'd like some new clothes. The head tells me her name is Deb. She lives and works here.

"Three days on, four days off," she explains and leads me down the hall to a room with racks of clothing and a full-length mirror. Deb does everything as if she's done it a hundred times. She shows me fancy clothes that I don't want, then hands me jeans that are too big and too long. I roll the cuffs then try on shirts and sweaters. Deb offers me a sweatshirt, but it's tangerine. She finds a sweater that's gray and zips up the front. I wear it with the jeans.

"Here, try these." She tosses slippers at my feet.

A child must have left them. The slippers have smiling polar bear faces and little red bowties. A perfect fit.

There are no polar bears in Antarctica. It's easy to get mixed up about the North and South Poles, particularly if you've never been to either place. People think there are Eskimos and igloos there, but that's at the North Pole where it's warmer. If you lived in Antarctica, you'd go to the North Pole on holidays. You'd pack a Hawaiian shirt and flip-flops.

Deb's face looks at me while I check myself out in the mirror. Even with the lip, I look pretty. It's why I can shoplift, why men take me in. I fling my bloody shirt into the trash.

At dinner I ask for seconds and take two pieces of bumbleberry pie. No one has an appetite like mine. The woman sitting to my right, who just arrived, is crying real soft. It makes some people even madder when you cry. My father, after he slapped you, went nuts if you cried.

As soon as I'm finished, I clear the table, like they asked, and lug the dishes into the kitchen on a big plastic tray.

"You're helpful," says a big sturdy woman in a dress the color of wilted celery. The cook, or whatever she is, grabs the tray, sets it on the counter and smears the food off the dishes into the trash. She's no-nonsense. Gets the job done.

"I can do it." I point to the dishwasher.

"Have a bath or watch T.V."

"It'll make me feel better," I tell her.

"Suit yourself."

The dishes are easy to do. Everything is organized. There's a plastic wrap dispenser with a row of sharp, evil-looking teeth—you can rip off the right amount with one hand. After I wrap the leftovers and the pie, I look around for anything else I can cover with plastic.

The curtains in the kitchen look homemade and someone has stuck plastic magnets on the refrigerator. It's like being at home, but someone else's home, someone you've never met.

I slide back through the dining room into the living room, wearing the slippers Deb found me. The polar bears have cheerful expressions but I'll sew stern eyebrows on them to give them a more wary look—something that will say they are mine.

There are three couches and two armchairs in the living room, but none of it matches. It's a hodgepodge of colors and styles. There's also a television, an upright piano, a teak coffee table piled with magazines and pamphlets, and a sagging bookshelf loaded with paperbacks, encyclopedias, and self-help books. It's donated stuff. All of it has the look of something useless, something no one wanted anymore. On the walls are paintings of winter, farmhouses, and barns—no people, just vague scenes of deserted life.

I sit on one of the couches and watch television. I try not to make eye contact with the other two women in the room. One is young, maybe eighteen, with spiky red hair and bad teeth. She wears a sleeveless shirt and her bare arms are skinny like snakes. She smokes menthols and looks blasted. I wonder if I look like that, too.

It's no big deal to be here, but most people thinks it is. It's like a Motel Six, if you think about it, only it's free and they make you dinner.

The other woman is in her forties. She's sitting with her legs tucked beneath her, wrapped in an afghan. She looks comfortable, as if she's relieved to be here. I bet she has five noisy kids and an unemployed husband at home. I bet she doesn't miss them one bit. I watch *Jeopardy!* and mouth the answers.

Anyone can go to the North Pole. It's not really that cold most of the time. It's not even as cold as Bismarck, North Dakota. It's the South Pole that's really cold. People don't know this, they think the North and South Poles are the same, except that one is on top of the Earth and one is at the bottom. Not so. The coldest day at the North Pole is about the same temperature as the warmest day at the South Pole. That's why there are no Eskimos or polar bears living in the South Pole. The reason the South Pole is so cold is its elevation. Antarctica is a mountain range made of ice.

Deb finds me. "Lily," she says and leads me back into the reception area.

A policeman stands by the door. He's big, even for a cop. His hair is short, neatly cut, black and shiny. If he smiled he'd probably be handsome, but he does not smile.

"He wants to talk to you," Deb says and leaves.

"I need to go over your statement." His uniform is spotless and someone irons his shirts with spray starch. A thick leather belt circles his stomach. The belt has all this gear clipped to it. It must weigh a ton.

I already spoke to the police at the hospital. The ER doctor called them. I didn't tell them much. It's none of their business, in my opinion.

"Okay?" I say. I feel foolish wearing bear slippers talking to a man with a gun.

"Your boyfriend claims you stole his wallet, credit cards and cash. Is that why he hit you?" The policeman's eyes are so dark that they look black.

The fish in Antarctica are called Ice Fish. Their blood is clear, not red, giving them a ghostly white color especially around the gills. Fish and animals in Antarctica have a kind of antifreeze in their blood to prevent them from freezing solid.

"No. Look, I'll give it back. I needed the money for a cab." It's not true. I did take the money and Jesse caught me, but what difference does it make? I mean the order of things?

The policeman writes in a tiny notebook—he even has a little pencil. He acts like he's writing something important, but he's probably making a list of things he has to do when he gets off work—pick up the dry cleaning, buy milk, call his mother.

I sit on the edge of the chair in my slippers and too large clothes. Crying might help so I sniff and wipe my eyes with a tissue. I touch my lip like it really hurts, though it doesn't. It's just feels fat and numb.

"Get the wallet." He talks like I'm a bad kid and he's the principal.

The wallet is under the pillow in my room. There are thirty-four dollars in it that I was hoping to use for my bus ticket tomorrow. The credit card's useless. Jesse never paid his bills. I shove thirty bucks under the mattress.

"Here."

The policeman flips open the wallet and fingers the cash, pulls out the credit card, puts it back in. His hard eyes look into mine.

"Don't leave town," he says, but we both know I can do anything I want after he leaves. The steel door slams.

When I walk back into the living room the women stare. Did Deb tell them about the police? Why would she do that? Isn't that a breach of confidentiality or something? I can't stay in this room. I grab a *National Geographic* off the coffee table and head upstairs. Deb stands in the hallway. I look down. I can't trust her now.

"For you," she says and hands me a plastic bag.

I figure it's underwear, a toothbrush and those little motel-size shampoos so I toss it on the bed like it's nothing. But I have nothing and nothing to do, so I reach over and look inside.

There's a present wrapped in Christmas paper and a card with my name, my whole name, in fancy handwriting. When I have some money I'm going to hire a lawyer to change my name to Heather or Rachael, so it doesn't remind me of my mother. She was just like her sister, my foul-mouthed aunt, Arlene, who named her boys Billy, Bobby, and Brian.

Maybe that's why the women looked at me funny, because they got me a present and signed a card for me—and I figured it was because they thought I was a thief.

I tear open the envelope.

Dear Lily Lucas,

Welcome to McDougall House, a place without harsh words or harm.

This journal is for your thoughts and dreams.

Everyone signed their names and wrote things on the card like it was a high school yearbook. They scribbled something like "You go, girl!" or drew a happy face or a rainbow.

Attached to the journal is a pen. I use my new pen to make a list of people I could stay with. My list is one name long.

I draw a picture of Antarctica. The Adélie penguins are marching across an ice floe and then the leader dives into the water and there's a big splash. Off to one side, nearly hidden from the penguins, a leopard seal lurks. He's huge with a grinning evil face and round all-seeing eyes. The waters are dense with fish. I draw one happy penguin's head above the water—with a fish flopping from his mouth.

It's still early. I can't sleep and I'm hungry. When I slip into the kitchen, the big woman is setting up the coffee urn for the morning.

"I wanted some cocoa, maybe more pie if that's okay?" I say.

"Sure, eat up."

I open the fridge and cut a large wedge for myself. The woman points to packets of cocoa. I sit at a slick table and watch her haul a garbage bag to the back door. She slips on a winter coat. Her hand is on the doorknob.

"I could save you," she says.

"What?" I answer with pie in my mouth.

"With the love of Jesus."

"Oh." Him. I can't think of anything to say.

She props the door open with the garbage bag and roots around in her purse for her car keys. "He loves all sinners, if they repent."

"I don't need saving right now," I say. "Maybe later?"

"We all need saving, dear," she says before she leaves.

"Yes," I say to the empty room. "Please save me."

The lowest temperature ever recorded was minus eighty-six-point-nine degrees Celsius at the Russian Volstok station in Antarctica, near the Southern Pole of Inaccessibility. There is also a Northern Pole of Inaccessibility, but it's easy to get to. You can even get there by dog sled, something you could never do in Antarctica.

The only person on my list, the only one I can think of to stay with, is my second cousin, Vicki Lynn. She lives in Eugene, Oregon, and I bet she'd let me stay for a week. I'll be helpful, like I always am, wash dishes, scour the bathtub, stuff like that. She has two little kids, so I know she could use help around the house.

But it won't last long and I always know it's coming when they stop making eye contact. Her broad-backed husband, Craig, will hand me a bowl of watery mashed potatoes but keep looking at his plate. Then Vicki Lynn will let her eyes dart around the kitchen while we sit and drink instant coffee.

After two days or maybe three, I'll hear them arguing, the sound muffled by the bedroom door of their manufactured home. Her voice will be hard to make out. She'll be trying to talk low, but I'll hear her husband say, "She's got nowhere to go because she steals from everyone who..." then "She's not troubled, she's *trouble*." Vicki Lynn will make a kind of pleading sound, like a squirrel, and then he'll go on about how I'm a grown woman and should get a job and stop sponging off everyone.

The next day she'll talk to me after dinner, when her kids are finally in bed and Craig's asleep. We'll be on the sofa bed, staring at the fireplace, and she'll tell me about a friend of hers who has a drycleaners, or manages a grocery store, and might need someone who's a real good worker. She'll offer to call them the next day. I'll pack in the morning, ask to borrow money, and promise to pay it back when I get a job.

At the South Pole there are only two 'days' in the year. For six months, the Sun circles the sky just above the horizon. After it tires, it sets and sleeps. For the next six months, Antarctica is plunged into a seemingly eternal darkness.

In the morning I'll call Vicki Lynn, tell her where I am, how Jesse slapped me around. Though I might leave that part out. It's hard to know what she'd think. Craig would think I had it coming. Like the cop, he'd assume I'd stolen the wallet and that Jesse was just getting back what was his. Craig would take Jesse's side for sure. No, I'll leave that out. I'll just say I'd like to visit, that I'm passing through. I won't tell them anything.

The Gregory O'Donoghue International Poetry Competition

Judge: Mary O'Donnell

1st Prize:
€2,000
Publication in *Southword*
Guest reading at the Cork International Poetry Festival
(with four-night hotel stay and full board)
Featured on the Southword Poetry Podcast

2nd Prize:
€500
Publication in *Southword*

3rd Prize:
€250
Publication in *Southword*

Ten runners-up will be published in *Southword*
and receive a €50 publication fee

The competition is open to original, unpublished poems in the English language of 40 lines or fewer. The poem can be on any subject, in any style, by a writer of any nationality, living anywhere in the world.

Deadline: 30th November, 2023

Guidelines: www.munsterlit.ie

Aneas

If you are curious about the best of contemporary Irish-language literature, we also publish *Aneas,* the only literary journal in Ireland exclusively in Irish. Published yearly, and including poetry, short stories and in-depth reviews, *Aneas* is available directly from us at munsterlit.ie/aneas and local bookshops. Issues can also be ordered from any bookseller who has an account with ÁIS.

Contributors

Devon Balwit walks in all weather. Her most recent collection, *Spirit Spout* (Nixes Mate Books, 2023), romps through Melville's Moby Dick. For more of her work, visit https://pelapdx.wixsite.com/devonbalwitpoet

Faye Boland won the Robert Leslie Boland Prize 2018 and the Hanna Greally Award 2017. She was highly commended for the Desmond O'Grady Prize 2019. Her first poetry collection, *Peripheral,* was published in 2018.

Despy Boutris is the author of the fiction chapbook *Burials* (Bull City Press, 2022). Her poems have been published in *Copper Nickel, Guernica, Ploughshares, Crazyhorse, Agni, American Poetry Review, Gettysburg Review,* and elsewhere.

Kevin Brown teaches high school English in Nashville, TN. He has published three books of poetry, a memoir, and a book of scholarship.

Madeline Beach Carey lives in Barcelona with her husband, son, and fox terrier. She teaches creative writing and is currently revising her first novel.

Ion Corcos has been published in *Cordite, Meanjin, Westerly, Plumwood Mountain, Wild Court, riddlebird,* and other journals. He is the author of *A Spoon of Honey* (Flutter Press, 2018).

Polina Cosgrave is a bilingual writer. Polina's poetry collection *My Name Is* was published by Dedalus Press. Her work has appeared in *The Stinging Fly, Crannóg, Banshee,* and many more.

Craig Cotter was born in 1960 in New York and has lived in California since 1986. His fourth book of poems, *After Lunch with Frank O'Hara,* is currently available on Amazon. www.craigcotter.com

Originally from County Cork in Ireland but still living in Spain after many years, **Jerm Curtin** received the 2021 Patrick Kavanagh Award, as well as the 2020 Cúirt International Festival of Literature's New Writing Prize for Poetry.

Monique Debruxelles is the author of four story collections and co-author of three crime novels. Her fiction has appeared in English in *The Southern Review, ANMLY,* and *Another Chicago Magazine.*

Patrick Deeley's eighth collection with Dedalus Press, *Cloud Ireland,* will appear in Spring 2024. A collection of surreal verse, *Beyond the White Deckchairs,* is due from SurVision also in 2024.

Ian Fisher's first byline appears in his own birth notice: Ian's newspaperman father had borrowed his name. Ian's next six bylines appear above *des contes* in England, France, and Canada.

Anne Freier is a writer and medical editor. She's currently crafting debut collections of poetry and short stories. Her work has appeared in *Miracle Monocle, Passengers Journal, Elevation Review,* and others.

Jake M.M. Griffin is a multimedia creator from the Northside of Cork City. His poems have appeared in *The Outpost Eire, Flotsam Mag* and *Tower Magazine.* @jake_griffin_is_lost

David Harsent's twelve collections have won numerous prizes, including the Forward, the Griffin International and the T.S.Eliot. His writing for the opera stage, in collaboration most often with Harrison Birtwistle, has been performed at major venues worldwide.

Paul Ilechko is a British American poet who lives in Lambertville, NJ. His work has appeared in many journals, including *The Bennington Review, The Inflectionist Review,* and the *Tampa Review.*

Pat Jourdan, former winner of the Molly Keane Award and Cootehill Poetry Award was second in the Michael McLaverty Short Story Award. She has published 5 novels, 4 short story collections and 7 poetry collections.

Anne Kennedy specialises in acrylics and watercolours. Her work is available at Passage West Creates.

Noel King was born and lives in Tralee, Co Kerry. His poetry collections are *Prophesying the Past* (Salmon, 2010), *The Stern Wave* (Salmon, 2013) and *Sons* (Salmon, 2015) and *Alternative Beginnings, Early Poems* (Kite Modern Poetry Series, 2022).

Sandra Kolankiewicz's poems and stories have appeared widely in literary reviews. Her most recent chapbook is *Even the Cracks,* which is forthcoming from Finishing Line Press in November 2023.

Christopher Konrad is a Western Australian writer and has many poems and short stories published including several books of poetry and a collection of short stories, *The Voyeur* (Balboa Press, 2021).

Heather Laird is a Lecturer in English at University College Cork, and has been writing creatively since 2021. She has been shortlisted for the MMCF Writing Competition and published in *Elsewhere: A Journal of Place* and *Crannóg.*

Anthony Lawrence's most recent collection of poems is *Ordinary Time* (Pitt Street Poetry, 2022), a collaboration with Audrey Molloy. He teaches Creative Writing at Griffith university and lives on Moreton Bay, Queensland.

Mercedes Lawry's most recent book is *Vestiges* from Kelsay Books. Her book *Small Measures* is forthcoming from ELJ Editions, Ltd. in 2024. She has also published short fiction.

Chin Li was from Hong Kong but now lives in Edinburgh. He worked as a clinical psychologist for years before focussing on poetry and fiction writing as a second career.

Elizabeth Loudon's debut novel *A Stranger In Baghdad* is published by Hoopoe Fiction, and her poetry has appeared in the *Saranac Review, Blue Mountain Review, OneArt* and *Trampset,* amongst others.

Michael Martin is a poet, editor and filmmaker living in North Carolina. In 2020 he was a finalist for Poetry International's Cavafy Poetry Prize. His first collection of poetry, *Extended Remark* was published by Portals Press.

Patrick McCusker spent several years working in British Columbia and in Ontario. He spent four months in a First Nations village where he obsorbed some of their understanding of nature.

David McLoghlin's third collection, *Crash Centre,* will be published by Salmon Poetry in May 2024. His work has recently appeared in *Howl: New Irish Writing* (2023) and elsewhere.

Mary Morrissy is the author of four novels, *Mother of Pearl, The Pretender, The Rising of Bella Casey* and most recently *Penelope Unbound,* and two collections of short fiction, *A Lazy Eye* and *Prosperity Drive.*

Lagnajita Mukhopadhyay Lagnajita Mukhopadhyay is an Indian-born author of the books *this is our war* (Penmanship Press, Brooklyn, 2016) and *everything is always leaving* (M.C. Sarkar & Sons, Kolkata, 2019), and poetry album *i don't know anyone here* (2020).

Lisa Mullenneaux's poems and essays appear in UK and US literary journals. She specializes in the translation of modern Italian poets and authored the critical study *Naples' Little Women: The Fiction of Elena Ferrante.* More at lisamullenneaux.com.

Laura Nagle is a writer and translator from French, Spanish, and Irish. Her translation of Prosper Mérimée's 1827 hoax, *Songs for the Gusle,* was recently published by Frayed Edge Press.

Massimiliano Nastri, born in the south of Italy, grew up in a German-speaking village up on the Alps. Temporary lecturer at Queen's University, he is currently re-reading Anne Carson and Bachmann.

Dan O'Brien is a poet, playwright, and nonfiction writer. His latest books are *Survivor's Notebook: Poems,* and *From Scarsdale: A Childhood.* He lives in Los Angeles.

Irish-Australian poet **Nathanael O'Reilly** is the author of ten collections, including *Dear Nostalgia, Boulevard, (Un)belonging* and *Distance.* He is poetry editor for *Antipodes: A Global Journal of Australian/New Zealand Literature.*

Triin Paja is the author of three collections of poetry in Estonia. Her first chapbook in English, *Sleeping in a Field,* is forthcoming from Wolfson Press.

Andrew Payton Andrew Payton is a writer, teacher, learning designer, and climate advocate living in Harrisonburg, Virginia with his partner and children.

Cathy Power lives in the shadow of Croke Park, Dublin, where, since retiring from full-time work she is editing her first novel and doing a Masters in Creative Writing.

Matthew Carey Salyer is the author of *Ravage & Snare* (Pen and Anvil, 2019) and the chapbook *Lambkin.* His work has appeared in *Narrative, The Scores* and *The Common.*

Samuel Samba is an indigenous writer of poetry & other works of art. His works have been previously published or forthcoming in *Australian Poetry Journal, Australian Access Poetry, Hill Hoist Magazine* and elsewhere.

Nnadi Samuel (he/him/his) holds a B.A in English & literature from the University of Benin. Author of *Nature knows a little about Slave Trade* selected by Tate.N.Oquendo (Sundress Publication, 2023).

Jaric Sarmiento is an MFA candidate at the University of Alabama and the co-creator of 108webnovel.com. His writing has been featured in *No Contact, A Velvet Giant,* and *The Other Side of Hope.*

Mara Adamitz Scrupe is a visual artist, filmmaker, and writer. She has authored eight award-winning poetry collections and her writing has been published in literary journals worldwide.

Lorna Shaughnessy has published four poetry collections with Salmon Poetry, most recently *Lark Water*. She is also a translator and co-edited *A Different Eden: Ecopoetry from Ireland and Galicia* (Dedalus 2021). www.lornashaughnessy.com

Eleanor Ariadne Shaw was born in Hessen, Germany to British and Greek parents, and is currently studying at the University of York. "Amidst Fierce Flames" is her first official submission for publication.

Jeanne Shoemaker graduated from the Iowa Writers' Workshop in 2010. In 2013, she won The Pushcart Prize for her first published short story. She lives in Victoria, British Columbia.

Cassie Smith-Christmas lives in Galway. Her novel *The Absence of Light* was a winner in the IWC Novel Fair 2023. Her poetry has appeared in *Aimsir, Causeway/Cabhsair; Gutter;* and *Poets' Republic.*

Alyssandra Tobin is the author of *Put Eyes on Me Not Like a Curse,* published by Quarterly West in 2022. Her poetry appears in *Banshee, Poetry Northwest, Grist,* and elsewhere.

Heather Treseler is the author of the forthcoming poetry collection *Auguries & Divinations* (2024), which received the May Sarton Prize, and *Parturition* (2020), which received the Munster Literature Centre's Fool for Poetry chapbook prize.

Widely published in Australia and overseas, **Isi Unikowski** lives in Canberra, Australia. His first collection, *Kintsugi,* was published in 2022. His published poetry can be viewed at www.isiunikowski.net.

Patricia Walsh has published two novels, *The Quest for Lost Eire* (2014) and *In The Days of Ford Cortina* (2021), and one collection of poetry, *Continuity Errors* (Lapwing Publications, 2010).

Monica Wang has writing in *Electric Lit, Malahat Review, Banshee,* etc. She was shortlisted for the 2022 W&A Working-Class Writers' Prize. Taiwanese-born and Canadian-raised, she now lives in Europe.

Patrick Wright is author of *Full Sight of Her* (Black Spring Press). His poems have appeared in *Poetry Ireland Review, The North, Poetry Salzburg, Agenda,* and *London Magazine.*

Ellen Zhang is a physician-writer who has studied under Pulitzer Prize winner Jorie Graham and poet Rosebud Ben-Oni. She has been recognized by the DeBakey Poetry Prize and as a National Student Poet Semifinalist.

Lucy Zhang writes, codes, and watches anime. Her work has appeared in *Apex Magazine, Split Lip Magazine, CRAFT,* and elsewhere. Find her at https://lucyzhang.tech or on Twitter @Dango_Ramen.

How to Submit

Southword welcomes unsolicited submissions of original work in fiction and poetry during the following open submission periods:

POETRY

What to submit:	Up to four poems in a single file
When to submit:	1st January – 29th February, 2024
Payment:	*Southword* will pay €50 per poem

FICTION

What to submit:	One short story (no longer than 5,000 words)
When to submit:	1st February – 31st March, 2024
Payment:	*Southword* will pay €300 for a short story of up to 5,000 words

Submissions will be accepted through our Submittable portal online.
Visit www.southword.submittable.com for further guidelines.

Printed in Great Britain
by Amazon

31774875R00081